The Institute
By Thomas E. Montgomery

The Institute is a work of fiction. Names, characters, places and incidents are either the constructs of the author's imagination or are used fictitiously. Any resemblance to actual persons, living or dead, events or locales is entirely coincidental.

Copyright © 2013 Thomas E. Montgomery
All Rights Reserved

Cover Art and Design by
John-Thomas Montgomery

*To my wife for her love and support of
a grumpy author in the throes of creation.*

Table of Contents

Chapter 1: The Mission 1

Chapter 2: Grandma Go Boom 3

Chapter 3: In the Ward 7

Chapter 4: His Mission... 10

Chapter 5: The Dr. and the Senator 22

Chapter 6: Sylvie's Orderly 31

Chapter 7: Back in the Mission 34

Chapter 8: The Russian Awakes 41

Chapter 9: Dapper Gentlemen 47

Chapter 10: Sylvie's Father 53

Chapter 11: The Ward Again 59

Chapter 12: Jackson's Childhood 66

Chapter 13: Whiskey Tango Foxtrot 68

Chapter 14: Not Much of a Party 78

Chapter 15: Deja Vu 95

Chapter 16: Exotic Cuisine 97

Chapter 17: Sylvie Awakens 107

Chapter 18: Senate Intelligence Committee 114

Chapter 19: Senator and Mr. Vincent Again 122

Chapter 20: Dapper Gentlemen Again 124

Chapter 21: FBI at The Institute............................. 131

Chapter 22: Wissle Goes After Them 133

Chapter 23: In the Cabin in the Woods..................137

Chapter 24: Back at Dad's 159

Chapter 25: Comeuppance.....................................161

The Silver Shadow..167

The Institute was a top-secret organization in Maryland near Washington DC. Its mission was obscure. Even its existence was known to but a few. The buildings were white. The walls were white. The furniture in the wards was chrome and white. The support personnel were dressed in white.

Outside the grounds, The Institute was thought to be an expensive, privately owned sanitarium. Their patients, who were their operatives, were availed the product of years of technical advancements in covert processes. Their minds were cleaned before a mission and then imprinted with only mission critical data. No need to pretend. They were their cover identities. They had no knowledge to leak to the enemy. Once back from the mission, their minds were returned to a pre-mission state. Fool proof.

Jackson Jethro Lanski, an operative, went on missions for The Institute. There was a mystery girl, with no apparent presence of mind. Jackson was curious about her circumstances and investigated between assignments.

Chapter 1: The Mission

In the shadows, a dark clad figure squatted down unnoticed as the security patrol passed by. The smell of garbage wafted on the night air. In the distance, the yowls of cats on the prowl, caught up in their clamorous courtship, competed with the crash and clatter of the trashcans they knocked over. Up quick and quiet the shadow ran across the alley to the reinforced concrete wall.

The steel door looked impenetrable. Above it, one story up was a window. The noises of the night, covered the sound of the window opening and the shadow dropping inside a dimly moon lit, musty warehouse.

Across the floor and up the stairs in fluid motion, like a shadow in the moonlight. With only eyes visible through the ski mask, the shadow paused at the door and listened. No sound. Turning the knob and testing the catch. Unlocked. The shadow entered the office.

Overhead lights flashed on. A dumpy little man stood with a revolver behind the desk.

"Hands up. Don't move," he said. "What do you want?"

The dark figure showed no concern for the man's pistol and approached the desk. In a soft whisper said, "We can both live through the night if you do exactly as I say. I need to have what is in your safe. Give me that and I will leave and you will live. Don't and you will die and I will take it after you're dead."

"But, I have the gun on you."

"You should have already used it." With a flicker, the gun was gone and the man was on the floor, bewildered.

"Now open the safe and you may still live."

"But what I have in there is of no importance to anyone but me."

"Open it now. You and I are running out of time."

"I don't think I will."

"This is a do or die situation, if there ever was one. I mean it do it or die. Last chance."

"No, I won..." He crumpled to the floor.

"Always the hard way," the assailant said, looking down at him.

The assailant opened the drawers of the desk and searched the contents. Then looked under the blotter pad. "Here it is." Found the combination and entered it. As the safe door opened a mist sprayed out. With a gasp and exhale, the assailant fell back.

Chapter 2: Grandma Go Boom

Sylvania Silverman was six years old, when the black limousine drove up the dirt road. It stopped in front of the quaint little house that her father had built with the help of his tune in, turn on, drop out, buddies. A moment passed. The passenger door opened with a swish of positive pressure. An impeccable, low heeled, black shoe stepped out. Then, just the peak of silver hair showed above the roof of the limo. As the Lady walked around the back of the limo, she glanced down at her now dusty shoes with marked disdain and entered the yard with a stern, purposeful expression on her face. Sylvie sat in her little chair, in the front yard, playing tea party with her best imaginary friends. The Lady's expression softened when she saw Sylvie. She stopped, bent down and spoke to her, then stepped up on to the porch.

Sylvie's mother stood in the doorway, clutching the apron she wore over a tie-dye t-shirt and jeans. Her hair was pulled back tight in a ponytail, with a yellow kerchief as a headband. It couldn't hide her classic beauty or her resemblance to the Lady.

She found the courage to say, "Hello, Mother. Come in."

"Hello, Mandy. Sylvie is lovely. Even if she is soiled."

Mandy's anxiety turned to anger. "Soiled? She is a wonderful little girl. How dare you?" She said ready to fight. The old battle lines, quickly, redrawn.

The Lady's expression went from stern to confused. With a sigh, "I'm sorry, a poor choice of words. I only meant to say her beauty shines through the dirt on her face."

"I know you don't approve of our lifestyle or of Josh, Mother."

"Where is that Vagabond?" asked Mrs. Silverman.

"Josh is on a book tour. His book is doing very well. He's been a very good provider. In spite of what you think." It was a well-traveled and familiar verbal path to an emotional stalemate.

"I didn't come here to fight. I came to warn you." She paused. "The world has changed, so much. Your father has some very powerful enemies. They may try to get to him through you and Sylvie. You are all in danger." She sighed once more. "Please come with me. We can protect you and your family. Yes, and Josh, too."

Outside, Sylvie picked up her tea set, cleaned them off and carried them into her bedroom. She put away her dishes in the little China cabinet; her papa had built it for her for Christmas. Sadly, she knew she would never play with them again.

Mrs. Silverman, Sylvie's grandmother had left their quaint little house down the dirt road, greatly saddened by the unresolved conflict between her daughter and herself. Nothing she said ever seemed to be heard or said the way it was meant.

Mandy's set of values had changed. "It was in college." Mrs. Silverman thought. "She had started hanging out with those neo-hippies. Probably, smoking pot and worse. Rejecting everything from our world, but the trust fund. Then, she got pregnant and wouldn't marry the boy." The sad lady shook her head. "I don't have anything against the boy. He was a big strong boy. He appeared to be a hard worker, though, he was Chinese."

Mrs. Silverman would ride back to the city alone. She had not been successful in her endeavor. Mandy would not come to live with them. She said they were able to take care of themselves.

Mrs. Silverman smiled as she thought of her granddaughter. "What a lovely little child. Looks so much like Mandy, at her age." Those were her last thoughts.

The explosion of the car bomb, echoed across the fields and all the way to Mandy's house. "I wonder what that was," she said to Sylvie. Sylvie started to cry.

Two men came bursting in to the house. "Come with us quickly."

"Who are you? What is wrong?"

"We are of your husband's family. We are here to protect you. We must go now."

Sylvie started towards the door. "Come on Mommy, we have to hurry."

They hurried into a four door, four by four and took off across the field. On the dirt road a black suburban was coming to a stop. Shots rang out. The plang, plang of bullets hit the four by four as they bounced and dodged away.

Chapter 3: In the Ward

Jackson Lanski woke in the decompression ward. Began to notice his surrounds and sighed with relief. The support staff were attending him. His mission was a success. The details faded, as he lay there relaxing and decompressing.

Jackson walked out of his semi-private room and into the ward. He visited with the other patients of the Ward. He grabbed a handful of peppermint candy from the orderly station and put it in the pocket of his hospital robe, as he passed.

Many of the patients were near catatonic. Some missions carried a heavier toll. He slipped them a peppermint candy as he continued on around the ward.

At last, he saw the one he was looking for. She sat in a wheelchair by the window. Jackson approached her and said he was back. Nothing. She continued to stare out the window at the swaying trees. Jackson never noticed the attendant until he spoke. He said that she had been this way since her return. Funny, Jackson couldn't think of her name. He felt, he should know her name.

That night, back in his bed. Asleep, he tossed and turned in the throes of a nightmare. He was reliving his mission. He woke. A sigh of relief. He was in the decompression ward, with support staff to attend him.

Deja Vu?

Jackson walked out of his semi-private room and into the ward. He visited with the other patients of the ward. He grabbed a handful of peppermint candy from the Orderly station as he passed. Many of the patients were near catatonic. Some missions carried a heavier toll. He slipped them a peppermint candy as he continued on around the ward.

At last, he saw the one he was looking for. She sat in a wheelchair by the window. Jackson approached and said that he was back. Nothing. She continued to stare out the window. Jackson never noticed the attendant until he spoke. He said that she had been this way since her return. Funny, Jackson couldn't think of her name. He felt, he should know her name.

His attendant, Wissle, came up behind him and asked, "How's your decompression going? Is your brain crapping out on you? Having trouble with reality."

Jackson realized that he was stuck in a loop, but said. "No. I'm coming along, okay." No more shock treatment for him. He'd get out of it on his own.

He was used to handling things himself. Self-reliance was ingrained into him at an early age. He had a basic distrust of doctors, lawyers and news pundits. They had too much to gain from bad things happening. Yeah, if bad things happened, they may be needed, but, frivolous is a word that applies to each of those professions.

* * *

The head of The Institute, Doctor Einrich and Jackson's attendant, Wissle, met in the doctor's office.

"How is Lanski's decompression progressing?" Doctor Einrich asked.

"He says he's doing fine, but I'm not so sure. I think he is covering something."

"Have you seen any signs of slippage?"

"No. I'll keep an eye out."

"Do more than that. Watch him closely for a while. Monitor his movements."

"Okay, Doc. Do I get overtime?"

"Just do it during your shift."

"Anything else?"

"Yes, How is Silverman?"

"No change. What do you want to do about her mission?"

"Send in Lanski. We can kill two birds with one stone."

Chapter 4: His Mission

Jack snooped around the ward looking for info on the girl. First he found her name and then the location of her room. That night, he sat in her white pristine room and watched her, as she slept.

Lots of questions needed answers. *Where were his memories of her? Were there other memories missing as well?* "I'd better start writing stuff down."

Jackson became aware of the sound of approaching footsteps. He jumped behind a curtain on the other side of the bed. An attendant did a quick look in. He puzzled over the chair, out-of-place, then put it back and left with a shake of his head.

Jackson waited a few minutes, then cautiously returned to his own room. Questions still buzzing in his head. *What is she to him? Why does he care? Why all the caution?*

In his room an attendant waited.

He sprayed a mist in Jack's face.

"It's time for your next mission. We have everything ready to go."

* * *

Jackson looked over the mission file. His mission, should he choose to take it, was to find Agent Silverman, help finish her mission and bring her home. Finishing the mission was first priority and she was second.

He'd been with her on missions before. He liked working with her. She was as tough as they come. Quick witted and fleet of foot. A partner you could depend on.

He looked at the picture. With her dark hair in a pixie cut and dark brown, almost black, almond shaped eyes, she could have passed for an actress or a model. It was quite an asset in their line of work. Easily a distraction for the opposition. But right now he needed to follow her trail, finish the job and bring her home.

She disappeared in Tampa on the west coast of Florida, while looking for a deep cover spy, suspected to be from eastern Russia that came in through Cuba. He had volatile information and we needed it. Her last checkpoint was in Ybor City.

Ybor City, the Latin Quarter of Tampa for more than a century. Cuban cigar companies and Cuban restaurants, Cuban culture had been there long before Castro's reign. The Cosa Nostra was not as visible as it had been during Trafficante's time. The NYC mafia had taken over after Trafficante Jr. died and most of the old warehouses had been discovered by yuppies and turned into groups of condos. Although, a few were still being used as warehouses.

The rental car pulled up in front of the old warehouse. Jackson got out. Six foot three, 195 lbs, dark almost black hair, blue-gray eyes, dressed in black pants with a midnight blue shirt. A black Durham raincoat covered the bulge of the silenced 9 mil in his shoulder holster. He kept a backup, 25 semi-auto, up high on the inside of his right thigh. Men were hesitant to reach all the way to the top of the leg during a frisk.

He banged on the metal door.

After a moment, "Yeah? What ya want?"

"Que Pasa, Hector? Yo soy Juan."

"What? Who? I mean Que? Oh, Hell, is that you Jack?"

He opened peephole door and looked out.

"Hey, Jack. Come on in." Hector escorted Jackson back to the office. "Have a seat."

Jackson took a chair, spun it around and sat down across the table.

"I'm looking for Sylvie. Where was she when she last checked in?"

"Straight to it, eh? No, how's it going ? Or How you been?"

"Sorry, but Sylvie's missing and time is running out. 72 hours is critical. Where did you track her to?"

"Last contact, she was going to a warehouse off of Adamo Drive and 22nd street. I don't know the address, just know a broken streetlight was near it. There are four possible sites that fit."

* * *

The first two didn't look promising. One was a bottling company and the other was a recycling company. As Jackson pulled up to the third warehouse, doors slammed down, Spanish voices rang out in alarm. Jack jumped through the big door as it slammed down. The inside of the warehouse was filled with cars in different states of disrepair and dis-assembly. A chop shop. The rats scurried out of sight and into holes. Jack grabbed one as he ran by.

"I'm not a cop and I'm not INS, I need information and I need it now."

"Okay. Okay. Put me down. What you need?"

"A woman was looking around here a couple of days ago. What can you tell me about her?"

" Is it worth some cha-ching?"

"Maybe if you have something worthwhile."

"Yeah, she came around here asking if we knew of some foreigner from Russia or something. She had some cha-ching to pass around."

"Where did you send her? Where is the Russian now?"

"The warehouse is a couple of blocks over, in the middle of the block. But they are not there, now. Some dinero?"

"Don't be cute, it can hurt you. Where are they now?"

Jackson lifted the Cubano up on his tiptoes by his pants.

"Okay. Okay, I tell you."

Jackson checked the fourth location, just to be sure. The door was unlocked. He went in quick and quiet and stopped behind a stack of crates marked farm implements.

The place had a musty smell.

Then Jackson slipped over to and up the stairs.

The office door was ajar. Inside the safe was open. The contents scattered on the floor. A sick sweet residue hung in the air.

Behind the desk was a body. It was a dumpy little man, dead still, no outward sign of injuries.

No sign of Sylvie. Jack shifted through the papers on the floor. He jammed some in his pocket and got out of there.

The Cubano's directions took Jackson over the Platt Street Bridge and into Hyde Park. To an old two story house. He drove on past and into the parking lot of a little shop on the corner.

As dusk fell, Jackson sneaked back to the house. He went into the backyard. The neighbor's dog barked. He walked over to the fence and gave the dog a treat from his pocket. "Hey, boy. Good dog." The tail wagged. No more barking. Jack continued around the house, looking in the windows. He located two goons downstairs.

"Okay, now to find Sylvie."

An upstairs window threw a square of light into the backyard. Jack climbed on to the back porch roof. He sneaked a peek with one eye in the corner of the window.

Tied spread-eagle on the bed was Agent Sylvie Silverman. Stripped down to black briefs and tank top, she appeared unconscious. In a chair, backed to the wall a scruffy, forty-something goon sat leering at the crotch shot. Sylvie raised her knees just a bit and moaned. With another moan, her whole body shuddered. Then a prolonged quiver centered on her crotch, accompanied a louder orgasmic cry, "Oooh, Oh, Oh."

The guard couldn't take his eyes off the bed symphony. He went to her. His hand gently stroked her inner thigh. He never saw the glint in her squinted eyes. But Jack did. He was sure she looked right at him. The guard unbuckled his pants and dropped them to the floor. He crawled on to the bed. As he straddled her left leg and reached to pull her panties aside, Sylvie kneed him in the groin. He fell forward and his nose met her shoulder coming up, hard. He was out cold.

Jack opened the window. With index finger to lips, he entered like a cat burglar, untied Sylvie and tied the guard in her place. His pants still around his ankles.

"It took you long enough," she said. " Were you enjoying the view?"

"Not so much. I had other things on my mind," he said. "Nice job on the guard. I wondered how you were going to get untied, though. I considered waiting to see. Where are your clothes?"

"They threw them in the closet."

Next door the dog started barking. She quickly dressed. She grabbed the guard's gun and gave him a sleep aid with the butt of the pistol. "He should be out a while," she said. She put a pillow case over his head. They sneaked back out the window and on to the roof.

Voices and the smell of cigarette smoke came up from the back porch.

"That damned dog won't shut up," said a voice on the porch. "I've got a bullet that will muzzle him."

"Why we gotta go outside to smoke? Don't make sense."

"My old lady don't want us doing it in the house."

"But she smokes in the house."

"Go figure. Can't live with..."

"I'm tired of that dog. I'm going back inside."

"Yeah."

The dog's barking covered the noise of their descent from the roof. Jack gave the dog a treat. " Good dog." He wagged his tail and panted happily. Jack and Sylvie crossed to the neighbor's yard, out to the street and then to his rental car at the store. He drove south on Bayshore Blvd and pulled into the restaurant parking lot.

"Are you ready for some food? We can eat while we plan our next move."

"I could eat. I need the energy."

"Seafood or burgers?"

"Did you find the book?" asked Jackson. He dipped the shrimp in the sauce.

"Yes. It was in the safe. I snatched it as I passed out," said Sylvie. "Those Mafia types must have it."

"Then we have to go back."

* * *

The bedroom door opened. "What the ...? Hey, Boss, you better get up here, now." he shouted. On the bed, with a pillow case over his head and his pants around his ankles was Sylvie's recent guard. "What the Hell? I wish I had a camera." Bruno, the boss, came in, pulled the pillowcase off and shouted at the unconscious fool on the bed.

"Where's the broad? Dumb ass. Hey, wake up you stupid putz."

He slapped him around, but no response. "Sergio, go look outside."

"Okay Boss, but the dog ain't been barking since we went out for a smoke."

"Yeah, well, go look anyway. I don't want'a be the one to tell Mr. Vincent, we let her get away. It could be very painful."

Downstairs the dog started barking, as Sergio opened the door. And kept it up as he scanned the backyard and on to the front of the house. He checked the street in both directions, then entered the front door.

"Boss, no sign of her. What you want me to do about that idiot upstairs?"

"Leave him where he is. It serves him right. I need to make a few calls."

"You got El Cubano's Repair Chop. Waz'up?" said the voice on the phone.

"Santo, it's Bruno. I need you to let me know if that girl comes around there again."

"I did last time. Didn't I? I'm always ready to help the guys from NYC."

"Santo, any more word on the Russian?"

"The dead guy you found in your warehouse, where you got the girl?"

"Yeah, he was dead and she was out cold, when we got there. You know what happened?"

"Not me. I figured you took him out and grabbed the girl."

"Don't pin that on me. He was already dead."

"I'm just saying ... So, did the girl ice him?"

"There may be more to her than you'd think. She was tied spread-eagle to the bedposts and now her guard is tied to her bed with his pants down and a pillow sack over his head, in her place."

"Mierda. ¿Verdad? She did this? Maybe she did the guy."

"Who knows. Let me know if you see her."

Santo looked out at his crew, "No se nada. Mihos. Callado. Say nothing to no one, about the girl," he said. He sat down behind the mounds of car parts, paper and car manuals that nearly covered his desk and lifted a yellow booklet from the pile. Across the cover was a Russian title.

* * *

The sun was not quite up when the rental car pulled into the store parking lot. Sylvie and Jackson got out and sneaked back to Bruno's house. Jackson greeted the dog with a treat. "Hey boy, good dog." The light was out in the second floor window. Quiet and quick once more up on the roof and over to the open window. With a small, LED, penlight, Sylvie lit up the man tied on the bed. She entered and silently slipped over to the sleeper. She pulled the pillowcase off and covered his mouth.

"Make a noise and you die." she whispered. "Clear?" The man nodded.

"Where is the booklet?"

"I don't know about no booklet. Would you pull up my pants for me?"

"Not yet. I need the booklet. Maybe I gotta pinch a nut to get you to tell me where it is." Sylvie started to reach in that direction.

"Wait! Wait! I never saw no booklet. There wasn't one on you when we grabbed you. I'm telling you. I never saw no booklet."

"You know, I believe you. If you promise to be real quiet, I'll put your pants on and not kill you. But, don't make me come back here. Deal?"

"Yeah, you sure ya don't want to take advantage of me first? I mean." He smirked and cocked his head toward his privates.

She rolled her eyes, then popped him in the jaw. Out like a light.

Back in the rental car, Jackson said, "I'd have left his pants around his ankles."

"A deals a deal. So where's the book? Someone had to have been there, before these guys," she said.

"The chop shop knew where you went and who got you. Maybe they know where the book is."

Jackson drove to the chop shop. Early morning work traffic had not started. A light fog had rolled in from the bay. With it came the smell of salt air and decaying fish.

Santo opened the shop door thirty minutes before his crew was due to show up. He liked the quiet time, first thing in the morning. No wife, no kids, no crew, just him, a good time to think about his "Great American Dream." The booklet might move that dream along in a big way. Someone would pay big money for that. He just needed to find out who. It was in Russian, but he could tell it had names and places listed in it. "Somebody wants this book," he said.

"Yes, we do." Sylvie stood in the doorway. "Give me the booklet."

"Or what?" He started to reach under the desk.

"I wouldn't," said Jackson as he followed Sylvie through the door. He held a silenced semi-auto pointed at Santo. He had always been a slow learner. His right hand continued toward the gun holstered on the side of the leg-well.

Sylvie ninja-ed around the desk and disabled his right arm.

"Hey, what did you do to my arm?"

"The booklet," Jackson said, "You ready to die for it?"

"What booklet?"

"The one that you said someone wants."

Santo glanced at the pile on his desk. "Don't know what you're talking about."

"Too bad, it could'a been worth something, but now you're just dead."

"Wait, here it is." Santo reached with his left hand. Got the booklet from under a pile of papers and gave it to Sylvie. "Ought to be worth a couple grand to you."

"Don't push it. Be happy to be alive."

"What about my arm?"

"It'll wear off in a couple of days. Stay quiet, now." Sylvie smiled prettily and walked out. Jackson holstered his gun and followed her out.

Santo sat there with his right arm hanging limp, useless. "Damn, I should'a told Bruno about the book. I hope this don't mess up the shipment delivery. Could be trouble."

Chapter 5: The Dr. and the Senator

In Dr. Einrich's study, the unpleasant smell of old leather, musty books and denatured alcohol greeted the nose as the doctor greeted the well-dressed, gray-haired gentleman seated in the leather chair.

"This treatment worked better than we expected. It has given an outlet for a great many psychoses. Mr. Lanski, your son has exhibited personality changes and thought disorder accompanied by unusual and bizarre behavior. He has shown signs of schizophrenia. This treatment allows him to engage full in his role, while we direct him to the resolution of his root causes."

"But my son had no symptoms. How did this schizophrenia happen?"

"The pieces can be in place, quietly, for a long time and then be triggered by some unrelated trauma. But I don't want to trouble you with minutia. I will keep you posted on his progress."

The doctor rose. The meeting was over. Mr. Lanski was not happy nor ready to let it drop.

" I want my son out of here and back where I can monitor him."

"But, that's not possible at this time."

Doctor Einrich held the door open for Mr. Lanski.

"I'll be back, you won't stop me from getting my son."

Through the window the doctor watched Mr. Lanski walk to his car. A few moments later, on the phone, the doctor said, "Jackson Lanski's father may become a problem. No. Not yet. Let's see how it develops. Yes, we may have to, but not yet."

He hung up and watched as Mr. Lanski's car left the parking lot. A gray sedan exited after his car.

* * *

"Where to Mr. Lanski?" asked his chauffeur as they pulled out of the lot. The Senator sat back in the seat and tried to relax. "To the Office. I need to call in some favors," he said.

"Yes. Sir." They drove through the Maryland countryside. As they pulled on to the freeway, the chauffeur interrupted Senator Lanski's thoughts. "Sorry to interrupt, Sir, but it seems we have a tail. Want me to lose him?"

"What? No. Which one?" The Senator glanced back through the tinted windows. "No, keep him there. Let him follow us," he said. "Colburn, I changed my mind. Go by the apartment. Oh, and Colburn, are you armed?" he asked.

"Yes, Sir. I always am. Part of the job." Colburn pulled into the gated parking garage. The gray sedan drove on past.

"Wait by the Car. I'll be back down shortly."

"Maybe I should go with," said Colburn. " Just in case."

"No, watch the car. The security is good enough inside the building and we don't want anyone tampering with the car."

In his apartment, the Senator went to the telephone and dialed a number.

"NYC'S DELI, what can I do for you?"

"Hello, is the order for Vincent Lanski ready?" he asked.

"No, but you can pick it up in thirty minutes."

* * *

As they drove over to NYC'S DELI (Pronounced Nick's Deli), Senator Lanski explained to Colburn, "I picked up my 9 mil, while I was up there. I'm going to leave it back here while I go into NYC'S." The tall art deco sign flashed in vertical blue neon, *NYC'S DELI.* They parked and got out. The Senator said "You should stay in the car."

"No, I know this place. I'm here to protect you, I'll be fine." Colburn stayed at his back, as they entered the deli.

"Mr. Lanski, your order is ready. You can pick it up in the kitchen." The clerk behind the counter directed him to double swinging doors.

Colburn opened the right hand door for the Senator. The kitchen clamor of pots, pans and Italian voices came out with the smells of pizza, pasta and sausage subs. A cook looked up and pointed to the walk-in cooler. They walked on back. A *tough* stood by the door. He held up his hand to stop Colburn. The Senator held opened his coat as he nodded to Colburn. The *tough* opened the cooler door. The Senator went in. Sitting on a crate of lettuce, was Mr. Vincent, the head of the NYC'S DELI franchise. He had sandwich deli/lounge combos up and down the east coast from Boston to Miami. Of course, there was no truth to the rumor that he had mob ties.

"Senator. How are you? How's your family?"

" Mr. Vincent. I'm sorry to bother such a busy man. But, I have a problem."

"Tell me. I owe much to the memory of your grandfather. If I can help, I will."

"Here's what I was thinking," The Senator explained.

* * *

The Senator and his driver came out of NYC'S DELI with two subs and drinks in paper sacks. They got into the car and pulled out into traffic. The gray sedan pulled out down the block.

"They're still with us, Sir."

"Good, don't lose them, yet. Perhaps, we can give them something else to do."

He called his office. "Ms. Pierce, Would you connect me with the deputy director of the CIA, please?" "Yes, sir," she said. And after a moment. "He is on the line. Are you ready for me to transfer?"

"Yes, thank you," he said.

"Mr. Kappland, How are you doing? I haven't seen you in a coon's age."

"Cut the crap, Lanski. I never hear from you unless you want something. What is it, this time?"

"Jethro, my son might be in a jam. I don't quite know what to do. I seek your counsel."

"Yeah, sure. What's up? You know, I will help my godson, anyway I can."

"Have you heard of Doctor Einrich or The Institute? It's just over in Maryland."

"I might have heard of The Institute. Why? Is Jackson involved with them?"

"Yes, they say that he is schizophrenic and they're treating him. That isn't the Jackson, I know. I want him out of there," he said. "That Doctor Einrich worries me. He's not telling me everything. I want to know, what is going on in that place and I want another diagnosis of my son."

"Okay, Jack. That doesn't sound like your boy to me either. I'll check into it and call you, when I know something."

"There is some urgency, here. I can't wait long before I do something."

"I know you, Jack, but we have to be real careful. We need to know whose toes we're stepping on."

"They're already stepping on my toes. And I'm afraid they're stomping on my son's. They won't like me when I'm angry."

"Don't do anything until I call. Okay?"

"Appreciate it, Jethro." He disconnected. "Colburn, we need to be wary. Things are going to happen fast, once they start."

"Yes, Sir. I'm always wary. It's my job. Are you up for this? It's been awhile since you've seen this kind of action."

"My son is at risk. I better be," he said. He brought him up to speed, on what he requested of Mr. Vincent.

Medals of Valor from thirty years ago didn't mean anything, now. Sure, he went to the Congressional Gym a couple of times a week, hit the bag a little and ran a few miles, but he didn't fool himself into believing he was ready for combat. He was no "Gibbs." Although, he thought he could still handle most one-on-ones.

* * *

Jethro Kappland hung up the phone and began typing on the computer keyboard. He owed Jack Lanski, big time. Anytime he could help the Senator, he would, as long he didn't compromise his job ethics or national security.

They had fought through some nasty situations together, in the military. Each had saved the other's life, a couple of times. They cared little about the medals, they had received. They were longtime friends. Jackson Jethro Lanski was named after Jethro. He liked to call him, "Jack's son Jethro Lanski."

He had followed Jackson's military career with a sense of pride and a concern for his well-being. He cared about the boy. "Boy?" He must be in his mid-thirties, by now.

* * *

In the back of the limo, Senator Lanski answered his cell phone. "Yes? Hey, Jethro. Did you find out anything on The Institute?"

"What have you gotten into? This is some serious stuff. Above top secret. No one wants to talk about it, or the good doctor."

"Did you learn anything that will help me get my son?"

"Most of it is vague, conspiracy theory, Illuminati type, rumors. But there are, definitely, some serious power players involved, shadow types. There is a board of directors, but I don't have any names, yet.

Doctor Einrich came to the U.S. about fifteen years ago. Story has it, he had a revolutionary process for treating mental disorders. He's kept it close to his chest.

He started The Institute and they say he has had some promising success. Not much more information is out about him or The Institute. Not even here," said the Deputy Director. "However, I did get the blueprints for the place. You want them?"

"Yes, send me a digital copy. Can you find out who is on that board? And why the shadowy status."

"I'm still looking into it further. I don't like not knowing, who's doing what to whom. There are so many agencies out there now you need a program to tell the players. If this is another one, I want to know. You keep me in the loop on this."

"Thanks, Jethro." He hung up.

A gray sedan pulled up beside the limo. The Senator's cell phone rang.

"We're here," said the voice on the phone. "Mr. Vincent said that you're the boss on this. We're to do what you say."

"Good, we need to proceed with the accident. Do you have the two guys that tailed me from the institute?"

"Yeah, they're in the back out cold."

They pulled the cars into an alley. Two men got out of each vehicle. They opened the trunk of the gray sedan.

"Strip them. Dress them in these." Colburn handed them suits with identification in them.

"Put the one guy in the front seat and the other with the nice suit in the back of the limo."

"I want this to look like an auto accident. I don't want you to kill them. I want them in the hospital."

"The clothes got no blood on them. We'll fix that," he said and smacked the driver in the face with his pistol then the back seat passenger received the same.

"Okay, Sir, if you and your driver will get out of here, we'll setup the rest."

"Thank you, gentlemen. Call me, after this is done." Senator Lanski and Colburn walked out of the alley and hailed a cab.

* * *

In the ward, a patient sat watching a cartoon with the sound off. He turned the volume up during the commercial then back off for the Heckle and Jeckle show. Jackson gave him a piece of peppermint candy. As he watched the muted television, the patient unwrapped the candy and popped it into his mouth. A commercial. Sound up. Special bulletin flashed across the screen. Jackson turned back to watch the alert. A smiling woman in heavy make-up, said in a cheerful voice,

"Senator Lanski of Texas was involved in an accident, this afternoon. He is in intensive care in Fairfax Hospital. The Limo he was riding in was hit by an auto that ran a red light and then sped away. The car, which had been stolen, was found, abandoned, a few blocks away. More details at six. Now, back to the show, in progress."

Jackson spun on his heel and walked out of the ward. He had to get out of there and check on his father. He started planning his exit.

Chapter 6: Sylvie's Orderly

An orderly in white, walked into Sylvie's room. The morning sunlight lit up the pale yellow walls and the striped curtain, which went around her bed with a cheerful glow. He checked her vital signs on the monitor, checked her IV and softly, pushed her hair away from her face. He looked at the girl, lying there, helpless. Even in a coma, with hair cut short and the absence of beauty care products, she was a beautiful girl. The orderly would deny he had a crush on her, but he could not deny to himself that he had a soft spot for her. He cared.

A second orderly came into the room. "Let's get this bedding changed," said Sylvie's orderly. "And keep your hands off the girl, this time. No copping a feel."

"Ah, what's the harm? She don't know nothing."

"It don't matter if she does or not. You, leave her alone. I *will* hurt you."

With one orderly on each side of the bed, they started to roll her over. Sylvie's orderly grabbed the hand of the other orderly and pulled it off of her breast. He bent the wrist back as he straightened the guy's elbow, pushing him up on tiptoes. He tiptoed him right on out of the room. In the hall he said, "Do not ever touch her again, perv, or, I will make you wish you were dead."

"Frickin' gook, another time. Another time." the orderly said to himself, as he walked on down the hall.

Sylvie's orderly vowed to keep an eye on the pervert. He was here to protect her. He finished changing the bedding by himself.

Jian Wang had been here since Sylvie arrived. Father Wang had assigned him to Sylvie after his brother, Wee, had been murdered. He took over for Wee. He would give his life to protect her.

It had been simple to start working at The Institute. There was a surprising lack of security for the agency it was rumored to be. He had forged an orderly's ID card and gone to work. He didn't get paid, so, no official inquiries came out of H.R. He was just a new orderly. Not uncommon. Things went on, which, he knew nothing about; but, it didn't concern him. He took care of Sylvie, exclusively. Day and night he guarded her.

The pervert orderly was walking along muttering to himself. When he came upon the cleaning girl mopping the floor. She got down on her hands and knees to scrub a stubborn spot with her scrub brush. She pretended be unaware of his approach.

Nice ass. He thought as he invaded her space. Here was an opportunity for a quickie.

"Hey, sweet thing. Want to make the big man happy? And I do mean big."

"What? So sorry. My name Lucy. No Swee Ting. No understand. What mean?" She turned and looked up at the pervert.

He reached down grabbed his crotch. "How bout, while you're down there cleaning, you clean my pipes?" he said with a leer. He didn't realize how deep he had stepped in it.

She smiled. "Can do. You come." She got up and headed to the cleaning closet. He followed. He couldn't believe his luck. That line had actually worked. His euphoria was short lived. In the closet among the shelves, she turned to him and grabbed his crotch and squeezed way too hard. "Like this?" she asked.

"Easy. Easy. Ow. Ow. Stop. Please stop." He was up on his tip-toes, again.

The cleaning woman smiled. "Take your pants off," she said. He did. He was a slow learner.

"Now your underwear." *Really slow*. He was grinning in anticipation, when she hit him in the side of the neck with a quick chop. Out instantly. She stuffed his underwear in his mouth then taped his mouth, wrists and ankles. That would keep him out-of-the-way, for a while.

She went back to scrubbing the floor.

Chapter 7: Back in the Mission

"Sylvie, do you have any idea what was in those crates back at that warehouse?" asked Jackson. "They were marked Farm Implements."

"No. I went in and straight up to the office. I planned to check them, on the way out."

Jackson took some papers out. "I found these on the office floor. Invoices for crates from Colombia. We need to check out those crates."

* * *

In the warehouse, Sergio said, as they carried the body of the Russian down the stairs. "Boss, what we gonna do about the girl? She may know about the shipment."

"Worry about getting rid of the body, now. We'll worry about the girl later," said Bruno. "Dump him in the ship channel. Get that putz from the house over here to help. Then start moving the shipment. Call the distributors, tell them it's in."

"Okay, Boss. What's that?" Sergio stopped, still holding the body. "Man! This is a spooky place. That came from over there." They dropped the body and drew their guns.

From behind a crate, out of the shadows, Sylvie stepped into the light. "Hi, boys. Cleaning up a mess?" She smiled. "What's in the crates?"

Bruno surprised but not overly concerned, said, "You don't wanna know. It would be unhealthy." He stepped closer. "I liked what you did to that putz, Dino, in the bedroom. I'm curious. How'd that go down?"

"He was distracted by my charms, but he 's still alive, or he was when I left him."

"Thank you for that. Unfortunately, I need him. So, you here for something?"

"Yeah, What do you know about the dead guy?" asked Sylvie.

Bruno said, "The Russian? He was dead when we found him. What were the two of you doing in our warehouse?"

"He got on with your shipment from Colombia when the boat stopped in Cuba. I caught up with him here. I had to stop him before he passed on some dangerous information to the bad guys."

"What information?"

"You don't know? Then you don't wanna know. It would be unhealthy," Sylvie said then smiled. "But enough about me, what are you going to do now?"

They still had their guns trained on her. Sergio looked at Bruno.

"Boss?"

"I'm thinking. I'm thinking."

"Oh, I should tell you. I do have backup. There are two guns on you as we speak. Notice the red dots on your chests," again she smiled. "Please place your guns on the floor. I'd hate to have to kill you after such a pleasant conversation."

Bruno looked at the dots, then nodded to Sergio as he put his gun on the floor.

"I'll want that back. Sentimental, Colt 1911, used to belong to Lucky Luciano. My dad gave it to me."

She admired the 1911 as she said, "Now your backups."

They removed their backup pieces and kicked them to her. She used zip ties to bind their hands and feet, then walked over to a crate and removed the two laser pointers from the top. She showed them to the bound pair on the floor.

"These pointers are quite handy," she said.

Upset, Sergio struggled with his bindings. Bruno just looked at her. "I think I'm in love. I see the putz may not be such a putz after all."

In the shadows, Jackson put away his laser-sighted pistol and smiled.

Sylvie disappeared into the shadows. The nails screeched as Jackson opened a crate of farm implements. Inside were packages of white powder. He took one package with him as they left the warehouse.

* * *

Jackson pulled up to the warehouse, back in Ybor City. He got out and banged on the big metal door.

"Yeah? What ya want?"

"Que Pasa, Hector? Yo soy Juan."

"What? Who? I mean Que? Oh, Hell, is that you again, Jack?"

He opened peephole door and looked out.

"Hey, Jack. Come on in. How did the mission go? You find Sylvie?"

He opened the door. He saw Sylvie, then.

"Sylvie, you're back. Glad to see you."

Sylvie nodded as she entered, but said nothing. Jackson gave her a puzzled look and spoke. "I have some powder which I need analyzed. Can you get it done for me?"

"Sure, give it here."

Jackson handed him the one-kilo package. "How soon can I get the results?"

"Right now," he said. He opened his knife, cut a slit in the package, took out a sample on a finger and tasted, then rubbed it on his gums.

"Wait." Jackson made an attempt to stop him. "I guess it's not toxic, then. I thought it could be anthrax. I wonder about people that taste things to determine the identity of a powder." Hector rolled his eyes. "Na," he laughed. "It's coke. Really good coke. My guess it's some of the best around."

"It only takes being wrong once. Hector. Setup a raid on that fourth warehouse site. There are at least three crates there that might be filled with coke. It's your bust. We'll head back to the Institute, Adios."

Back in the car, Jackson turned to Sylvie, "You have a problem with Hector?"

"Yes, maybe I do. No one knew I was going to that warehouse, except Hector. And yet, the trap was setup and waiting."

"Perhaps the trap was set for someone else."

"Yeah, we'll see," she said, playing with the Colt 1911.

* * *

Hector picked up his phone and called.

"Hello," a woman's voice answered, a slight New York Italian accent.

"Better send someone to the warehouse, Bruno's got trouble and not much time."

"Who is this?" she asked, but phone was already dead. She hurried upstairs. The putz was sleeping, hands and feet still tied to the posts.

"Wake up, Dino, Wake up," she slapped him hard. She cut the zip ties off his ankles.

"Hey, I'm awake. Oh, hi Lucia. Where's the Boss? We got time for some head-to-head?" he said with a smile.

"No, we don't. Bruno is in trouble down at the warehouse. Get down there, now." She cut the zip ties off his wrists. She gave him a cold look. "Don't make me regret our little tête-à-tête. Now take your little sword and get your ass down there. Tell him, I got a phone call, a warning."

"Little? Okay, okay, I'm going."

Bruno and Sergio had not been idle. They had gotten the zip ties off their wrists and were working on the ankles went Dino arrived at the warehouse. When he came inside, Bruno was behind the door. He jumped him and wrestled him to the ground.

"Dino, it's you." He let him up. "What are you doing here?"

"Your missus got a call. A warning saying you were in trouble."

"From who?"

"They didn't say. Just the warning, then hung up."

"Okay, we need to get the coke and get out of here, now. The Narcs know about the shipment. Bring the cars around."

* * *

The sirens burst through the afternoon. A Swat truck, squad cars and black SUV's screeched to a stop on all sides of the warehouse. The men, with military precision, erupted into the warehouse, shouting, "DEA. You're under arrest." Then, "Clear." "Clear." Up the stairs. "Clear." "Clear."

The team milled around in the warehouse. A Swat team Sergeant said to the officer in charge. "There's no one here, sir. The drugs are gone. Just empty crates."

"We're too late." The officer in charge said to Hector, "Perhaps, you were a little slow at calling us. Is that likely, Hector. Were you sleeping or what?"

"What? Don't blame me. I called as soon as I heard. Hey, I'm out of here." Hector turned and walked out to his car. He smiled as he thought of the kilo of coke he had stashed.

* * *

Bruno had called his distributors and gotten the coke into their possession. "Don't step on it more than twenty-five percent. We got a reputation," he told them.

Sergio and Dino carried the Russian to the car and drove across Adamo Drive on the 22nd Street Causeway to a run-down wharf. There they dumped him in the ship channel and drove back to Bruno's house.

Chapter 8: The Russian Awakes

The chill of the water caused a strange reaction on a dead man. The shock caused him to regain consciousness. He struggled to the surface and with a sudden gasp of air, looked around. *Where was he? What had happened?* He slowly swam to the shore and climbed on to the rocks. He looked around. Nothing was familiar. *Tampa, USA, That's it. The cook said he had a nephew. The letter?* He took it out of the water proof pocket that held his papers. *Not too wet. Where was the shop? Here's the address.*

He started walking up the causeway. In his soggy clothes and squishy shoes, it was likely that he had a long trek, before him. Ahead, he saw the docks and the boat he had come in on. A taxi sat waiting for a fair. He quickly got in and shut the door. "Here," he said and showed the address on the envelope. His English was as bad as his Spanish, but both were borderline understandable if he took his time.

Santo was struggling to close the shop doors, when the taxi pulled up. He turned to see a soggy dumpy little man step out of the cab. The man held up his hand and said wait.

Santo said, "We're closed," as the man came up to the door.

Boris said, "You Santo, nephew of Alfred, ship cook?" he asked. He got out the letter.

"Yeah, who wants to know? Is he alright?"

"My name Boris. I have letter," he said and handed over the letter."

The taxi driver honked the horn. Boris held up his hand and signaled again to wait.

Santo scanned the letter. "My uncle speaks for you. He likes you."

Boris looked at the taxi. "You change pesos to dollars for taxi, yes?"

Santo gave the driver a bill. "Keep the change."

The taxi driver drove off. "Humph. Big spender," he said out the window.

Santo reopened the door. He and Boris walked into the dingy break room. Boris' shoes made squishy sounds with each step. Santo turned on the light and got a good look at Boris.

He jumped back. "Dios Mio," he said. "You are that dead guy."

"I don't understand. Nyet. Not dead. Wet. I need clothes. Bag in warehouse."

"You sure looked dead in the warehouse. What happened to you?"

He told Santo about the quick and deadly attacker.

Santo laughed. "That attacker was a girl," he said. "She's bad news. I haven't moved my right arm, since she poked me. The less I have to deal with her, the better."

"A girl? She was good, fast. A girl." Boris shook his head. Russian women in the KGB might be that good, but an American? Not what he had been told.

"My book, you see my book? I need my book. I have plan."

"Yes, I found the book with your body."

"You had book?" asked Boris. "Where is book?"

"Yes, I had the book, the girl took the book from me."

"Where is girl? I need book."

"I will check around. You can stay here." Santo showed him the room next to the break room. It had a cot with a ragged blanket and a dirty pillow. It was as dingy as the break room. "This is it. You are welcome to use it."

"Thank you. Is good."

* * *

Hector drove back to his Ybor city warehouse. The coke would go in his retirement fund. He was working on a plan. He needed to convert the coke into money without Bruno or Mr. Vincent finding out. Maybe on the west coast. He had a street contact in L.A, but getting it there could be a problem. Maybe, he would FedEx it to her. When he arrived at the warehouse, he would give her a call.

"Chareese, how are you doing? Are you keeping that booty warm for me?"

"Who is this? Hector? Hey, how you doin? Yeah, I been missing suma dat," she said. "What you up to? Where you been?"

"Listen Chareese, I got something I need to move. You might want in."

"Word. Folks are always tagging my cell. I'll call you back, when I can, kay?"

"Sure, tick tock. Later."

"Bout an hour. Bye."

Hector thought to himself, *Maybe I should test that stuff for quality.* He smiled at his little joke. He took a single-edge razor blade and laid out some lines from a small vial, on the table. "Just a couple," he said, but, two became four, became six. "Ah, the tingle." He sat back with his eyes closed, enjoying the euphoria. Unfortunately, his timing was not the best.

Sylvie and Jackson had heard that the bust had not been successful. That the warehouse was empty. This might have been Hector's doing. Sylvie still suspected he had set her up. She decided to pay him a visit. Since, Jackson was involved in tracking down the coke shipment. She would go alone. She didn't need his help to handle Hector.

Slick and slow, a fleeting shadow moved across the warehouse floor to the office door. Inside, Hector sat with his back to the door, bent over, smelling the table through a rolled dollar bill.

Sylvie entered and stood at his right shoulder. "Don't let me interrupt your fun," she said. Hector started and spun around in the chair. "What the … Don't do that for god's sake. You'll give me a heart attack," he said. "What do you want? Your mission a success? What you need from old Hector?" He was thinking sex and coke was a killer combination and she was a real knockout. He should have been looking at her eyes, instead. They were very cold, like chunks of black ice.

"You want a little, snort?"

"Maybe later. I have a couple of questions, I want answered." She put her hand on his shoulder and turned him back to the table.

"Sure, what you need to know?" he said, looking over his shoulder at her.

"Who did you tell that I was going to that warehouse?"

Hector thought he was thinking fast and clear. "I didn't tell anyone, that. I just ..."

"What did you tell and to who? Think this out. Hector, this may keep you alive."

Hector knew she would and could carry out the threat.

"I just warned Bruno and his crew that the bust was coming to the warehouse. I didn't say anything about you going there, I swear."

"Why didn't you tell me who that warehouse belonged to?"

"I didn't know that you were going there. I only knew that you were going to the chop shop. Maybe they informed."

"So how long have you been a mole for the mob, Hector?"

"I'm not a mole. I just ..." Hector looked over his shoulder, she wasn't there. He turned around in the chair, she was not in sight. She was gone. "Spooky."

Hector sat at the table. He needed just a touch to replace the high that Silverman had taken from him. He spread out some lines and sucked them in.

He leaned back. "That's better. Much better," he said. The phone rang. He picked it up.

"Ah, yeah, you got me. Waz'up."

"Hector, it's Wissle. How's the Silverman/Lanski mission coming?"

"Cool man, everything is cool. Too cool man."

"Are you high? What the shit. Are you crazy?"

"No, Man. I'm not high. I reconnected with an old girlfriend. I am just feeling good."

"Yeah, well. It's your ass. Have they got the book?"

"Yeah. They got it."

"Then gas them and ship them to us, ASAP. Clear?"

"Will do. Later." After he hung up, he called Lanski and said he had information on the coke. Then he called Silverman and told her he had information on the Russian. When they came in, he did as Wissle had told him.

Chapter 9: Dapper Gentlemen

In the paneled boardroom, of an exclusive men's club, dapper elder gentlemen sat around a long table of dark mahogany. The light from the green shaded lamps, reflected in the hand rubbed sheen of the tabletop, cast a soft green glow that matched the carpet and the casual money evident in the room.

A dignified group of self-assured men of understated wealth and power. The men behind *the men of power*. Seven men of seven ethnicities, together once again to deal with the problems of the Institute.

The smell of expensive cigars and old money invaded the senses of Doctor Einrich, as he stood at the foot of the table, waiting to be addressed.

"So, Doctor. What progress can you report? Have we got the book?" said the gentleman on the end.

"We have had great success with the mission scenarios. We will have the book shortly. That mission is nearly complete," he replied.

"What is the cause of the delay? We have heard, shall we say, rumors that some anomalies have begun to appear. That is worrisome. Don't you agree?" said another man at the table.

"Yes, there have been some anomalies, but the percentages of success have been very high. The program is going as predicted, within our margin of error."

"What of Ms. Silverman? Is she one of these anomalies?" asked the Asian man.

"No, not yet. We have sent in Jackson Lanski to extract her and bring out the book."

"You're playing with the mind of a sitting senator's son. Do you realize that? He could make it very difficult for us, if something were to go wrong," said the Austrian.

"I will take care of the Senator if it becomes necessary," said the doctor.

"See that you do. More than your program is at stake."

"Yes, the stakes are high, but the rewards have been as well. Destroying that book, before others can find out what it contains, would be of a benefit to you. Would it not?" The doctor nudged back at the gentlemen, just a bit.

"You should be careful, Doctor. Leave us. Bring us that book."

Doctor Einrich turned and walked out the ten-foot tall double doors.

After the doors shut, the gentleman at the head of the table said, "Perhaps the good doctor is feeling too assured of his position. He believes he is indispensable. Watch him. The Senator may not be the only one who is a threat." The Austrian acknowledged him with a nod.

* * *

Boris had been in the KGB. It had not been as romantic as it had sounded when he was recruited. Even the KGB had need of clerks and other desk bound personnel. Boris had dreamed of being out in the field, uncovering a spy ring or catching a corrupt administrator or a subversive dissident. Instead, he had sat at his desk sifting files from the in-box to the out-box, day in and day out. Boring, tedious work, he would check to see if the security status was marked appropriately. Was it top-secret? Did it need to be? Should it be lower or higher? One file changed his life.

The file had looked the same as all the others that paraded across his desk. A big red Top-Secret, in Russian, was stamped on the cover. Boris took the file off of the stack. Inside was a booklet titled, *American Assassinations, The Bay of Pigs and Other Covert Operations*. He remembered the Cuban Missile Crisis. In grade-school, he had hidden under his desk when the warning alarm signaled a practice drill.

He opened the booklet and scanned the pages. "Bozhe Moy," he said as he flipped the pages. Here were names of sleepers and locations of safe houses. He continued flipping pages. "Moy." He found details of the assassinations: The groups responsible and the names of those involved in the cover-up afterward. He wanted to read this.

He looked around at the other clerks at their desks. No one was paying him any special attention. He opened his desk drawer, took out his lunch pail, removed the remains of his lunch, then rolled up the booklet and put it in the pail. He would bring it back tomorrow. No one would know.

He had never brought it back and no one ever knew. He had forgotten it. Years later, he was looking through a box. Inside was his KGB identification, the contents of his old desk and the booklet.

He sat at the ancient chrome and mica kitchen table in the shabby apartment. He was hungry, but he had to wait. Boris had a government check which never made it to the next one; there was always a week of near abstinence. His stomach growled. He scanned the booklet, turning the pages slowly. An idea, born of hunger, began to form.

In the USA the information would be worth a lot of money. Maybe he could write a book or sell the story on television and not turn over the actual booklet.

The KGB ID cleared the way out of the country and on to a ship to Cuba. Once there, it was a simple matter to get on board a boat to Tampa. The plan might have worked, had he not been so eager to impress the lovely Cuban woman. He told her the contents of the booklet. She was a part-time snitch, as well as, the full-time hooker he had hired. For a few pesos, she passed on her knowledge of what he was carrying. He was already on the ship to Tampa, when the Operative removed the knowledge from her brain with a bullet to head.

Boris stayed pretty much to himself on passage to the Port of Tampa. He did acquire one friendly acquaintance. A Cuban cook who spoke Russian, but poorly. The cook enjoyed practicing his Russian on Boris. Boris enjoyed the chess games and conversations the two of them had on the three day trip. The cook had a nephew in Tampa. He owned an auto shop. When they arrived in Tampa, the cook had given him a letter to give to his nephew, Santo, and got Boris a ride in the delivery truck to a warehouse four blocks from the shop.

* * *

Doctor Einrich sat at his desk his head in his hands. The book had disappeared, before he had a chance to learn the information it contained. He was sure that Lanski had it. But Lanski's brain had been wiped and imprinted back again. The doctor had no way to force him give up the book. Lanski just didn't know.

He had looked at the security videos. *Lanski never had it, visibly, with him. Where was it? He couldn't ask Wissle. It was just best that he didn't know it was gone. Maybe Wissle took it. I'll watch him.* The thoughts kept churning around in his head.

He needed that book to solidify his position with the Board. Without it, it would be harder to leverage a better situation for himself. Not impossible, just harder.

The Board was referred to, in the book. And, of course, he would have to remove any reference to himself and the Institute. But he had to get the book back from Lanski. There was too much useful and damaging information to let it remain in anyone else's hands.

The doctor spun around in his chair. *Was that a Rat?* He called Maintenance. "Get someone in here and find this rat." He hated rats.

Chapter 10: Sylvie's Father

Sylvie's father, Josh Low was a fourth generation American. His great-great-grandfather had been brought here to work on the railroads. A Chinese coolie with an incredible work ethic, long before it was popular. Josh had inherited that work ethic even as he rejected other trappings of his culture. He had spoken Mandarin Chinese only when speaking to his grandparents. As a child, he had studied a martial art called the Iron Fist, made popular by Bruce Lee.

He had met Mandy Silverman in a creative writing class they took together. Mandy loved his poetry. She took a Mandarin Chinese class and convinced him to tutor her. They became friends then lovers. When she became pregnant they moved in together. They lived mostly on Mandy's trust fund, but Josh also brought in some income with odd jobs and tutoring. Then, he won a poetry contest. His poem was published and his writing career was launched.

After Sylvie was born, he began teaching Mandy martial arts. Mandy insisted they speak Mandarin on weekends and during training sessions. Sylvie was raised in a house with Mandarin and martial arts training. When she was two, her Papa started her with simple little fun things that began the muscle memory exercises of later on. By the time she was six she could speak two languages and could whip most ten year-olds. She rarely fought; her parents had not neglected her ethics lessons.

After, Josh disappeared, Sylvie's mother had continued her training. She was quite a prodigy and excelled far beyond her mother. When she got into her teens, Mandy let her go to Josh's martial arts master for more training.

* * *

Sylvie had just turned ten, when her father had disappeared. He had just published his third book and was going to New York, once again, for a book signing. He never made it there. She had never heard from him, again.

Josh's flight had taken him to a one-hour stopover in Pittsburgh. While he waited, he sat in the airport lounge sipping an Irish whiskey, neat with a water back. He was thinking about his mate and his little Sylvie. He wished Mandy would consent to a wedding.

He had been asking her since they had first got pregnant, but she was adamant in her refusal. She said their families would never allow it to happen or would make it very difficult for them if they went through with it.

Mandy never explained further. She would give him that look. The one that said, "Keep it up and you are going to piss me off." Josh knew to let it drop, again.

An Asian woman in a flight uniform, paused behind him.

"Excuse me. Are you Josh Low?"

He turned around, "Yes, I am."

"Please come with me. There has been an emergency at home."

Josh jumped up and followed. "What? What happened? What kind of emergency?"

"I don't know, sir. You will soon find out. Through here, please." She led him through the door, turned and locked it after him.

In the room waited three Asian men, one sitting behind a desk, two standing at each side. "Shee-yeh," he said to the attendant. "Thank you. You may go." She left the way she came in. He looked at Josh for a moment. "Your life has just changed dramatically. I'm sorry, but you will not be going to New York today. Your Tang calls you."

"What? I have to go. I have a book signing. I care nothing about the old ways. Who are you, anyway, to tell me this?"

"I am Mr. Wang. Think of me as your uncle. I am your mother's uncle. You are next in line to run our organization. Your family is now in danger. Our enemies will hunt down your family and kill them, if you don't leave them, now and disappear." He paused to let it sink in, then he looked down at the desk. "They killed my son and his wife and my three lustrous grandchildren."

"But, why me? I know nothing about the Tang or how to run it."

"There is no one else. You will be taught. You will leave for Xi'an, tonight."

"But, my family? I must tell them. They will worry." He stopped. It sounded weak even to him.

"It is best, that they never know. They will continue to be protected. Now we need to go."

* * *

For ten years, Josh had lived, studied and worked in Xi'an (Pronounced Shee-Ahn). His wife and daughter were memories of a happy time of long ago. The Tang had become his life. He learned its ways and means, the ins and outs of an international organization. There were legal and, in some places, illegal undertakings to be considered. He was given housekeepers, gardeners, guards and concubines. He had a large suite of rooms in the Weiyang Palace of his ancestors. The life was seductive.

He was groomed to take over when his great-uncle retired or died. He received regular reports of his family's life, along with the numerous reports of the Tang's business interests around the world.

Five years ago he returned to New York City. It was the center of operations for the Tang in the U.S. He had not tried to contact his family. Although, he continued to receive the reports and pictures. He smiled as he thought of his old martial arts master training Sylvie. She would have been a challenge for him. And he, her.

He thought of the book signings he had had in the city when he was happily only an author. At the last signing at a bookstore just off Wall Street, he had come close to being blown to bits. Only the timely shooting accuracy of a young sniper prevented the terrorists from killing him and many others.

The terrorists had brought a bomb into the store inside a box of books, the same store, in which, he was having the book signing. The sniper was a member of a terrorist task force monitoring that cell. Josh was held at gunpoint by one of the terrorists as they prepared to set off bomb. With one arm around his throat and the gun to his head, he thought it was all over. Then, blood sprayed from the forehead of the man holding him, before the terrorist hit the ground, the other two terrorists were shot through the head and fell to the ground, as well.

The task force and the young sniper rushed into the store. The leader of task force asked if everyone was okay. They were. Except the terrorists, of course. Josh introduced himself to the sniper. "Hi. My name is Josh Low. Thank you. You saved my life."

The sniper shook his hand. "Jackson Lanski, you're welcome." He looked at the dead bodies. "It had to be done," he said.

Chapter 11: The Ward Again

Jackson Lanski woke in the decompression ward. Began to notice his surrounds and sighed. The mission was a success. The details faded as he lay there relaxing and decompressing. The Support staff attended him and closely monitored his progress.

Jackson walked out of his semi-private room and into the ward. He visited with the other patients of the Ward. He grabbed a handful of peppermint candy from the orderly station as he passed. Some patients were near catatonic. Some missions carried a heavy toll. He slipped them a peppermint candy as he continued on around the ward.

At last, he saw the one he was looking for. She sat in a wheelchair by the window. This time Jackson held back. Now, sure he should not draw attention. He watched from across the room. She stared out the window. Funny, Jackson couldn't think of her name. He felt, he should know her name.

Wissle, his attendant, came up behind him and asked, "How's your decompression going? How's reality today? Having trouble."

Jackson realized his memory sucked, but said. "No. I'm coming along, okay." No more shock treatment for him. He'd figure it out on his own. He no longer trusted the staff of the Institute.

The specter of paranoia grew. In the Ward he watched the staff closely, for signs of betrayal. Or duplicity. Something was not right. Something was going on. He wasn't sure but he thought the girl was at the center of the storm. He was going to find out.

There were some residual effects from the imprints on Jackson's mind, which caused confusion between real and illusion. He had episodes of flashbacks into those past missions. They didn't last long. Sometimes just a few seconds. But, he knew he had to get away or lose his essence, his soul, his self. One day, he was afraid they won't be able to imprint him back on his brain. And he would not return from the mission and he would be one those nearly catatonic patients in the ward. After each mission, it took longer to integrate his conscious and subconscious.

* * *

The subdued light from the ward filtered through the blinds as Jackson dug into the doctor's office files. He found Sylvie's and his files, made copies and put them back. He studied the framed floor plan on the wall.

As he memorized the layout and the placement of the cameras, he looked for a way to leave the building undetected.

He tapped a location on the layout. He needed a place to hide the files where he could find them again, after they zapped his memory.

He busted a seam in the back of the doctor's couch and hid the file copies, then, pushed the couch back against the wall.

He made his way through the dim, deserted ward and into the girl's room. He sat and watched her toss, turn and twitch on her bed. Quite a dream. He heard the sound of approaching footsteps and slipped behind the curtain.

An attendant did a quick look-in. Puzzled over the chair, out-of-place, he checked the patient, the vital signs monitor, put the chair back and with a backward glance at the chair, left the room.

Jackson waited a few minutes as the echo of footsteps faded down the hall. Then he cautiously exited and returned to his room. Questions buzzed in his head. *What is she to him? Why does he care? What happened?*

* * *

"Well, Lanski is at it, again. He was caught on the security cameras snooping around last night. He went to see the girl, again." Wissle, the head attendant said.

The doctor said. "Send him on another mission. I know it is a little too early. When he returns index his memories back to his return from the last mission."

"Will do, Boss," Wissle said with a smile. "I like that."

* * *

On the security monitor, the guard noticed Jackson in a secure area. He called Wissle.

"Your boy, Lanski is in the Security hallway. You want me to apprehend him?"

"No, Culp. I'll handle it."

Wissle met Jackson as he came out of the Security hallway.

"Hey, Lanski. What are you up to? Not looking for trouble are you?"

"Just taking a walk. Is that a problem?"

He laughed. "It just don't matter. Soon, you won't remember anything about it, anyway, just like last time."

"What does that mean? What's going on?"

"You get back to your room. I'll stop by later and tell you about it."

Wissle stood and watched Jack walk done the hall. He chuckled to himself.

Jack considered what Wissle said. On the way back to his room he wrote some notes and hid them in an ac vent. Inside were other documents, he had hidden earlier.

In his room an attendant waited. As Jackson entered. The attendant said, "It's time for your next mission. We have everything ready to go." He sprayed a mist in Jack's face.

On a gurney, they took Jack into the Clean Room, a white room with electronic equipment on the walls all around the room and a slanted table with straps for feet, hands and head, in the middle of the room. A helmet with coiled wires, up and over to the wall equipment was suspended above the head strap. The straps were tightened and the helmet placed on his head. Zapping, cracking and buzzing sounds, like an old movie, filled the room.

* * *

Jackson Lanski awoke in the decompression ward. He recognized his surroundings with some anxiety. The support staff was attending him. His mission was a success. The details... *The details? There were no details, Fading or otherwise. What was the mission? What the foxtrot had happened?*

He lay there and searched through his recent memories, looking for the gaps. Determined to find what was missing.

Jackson walked out of his semi-private room and into the ward. He visited with the other patients of the Ward. He grabbed a handful of peppermint candy from the orderly station as he passed. Some patients were near catatonic. Some missions carried a heavy toll. He slipped them a peppermint candy, as he continued on around the ward.

He couldn't find the girl. He asked the attendant, "Where is the girl that is usually by the window."

The attendant asked, "Which one?"

Funny, Jackson couldn't think of her name. He felt, he should know her name. "Never mind. My mistake," he said and turned away. He went to her room. It was empty. No sheets on the bed, it was unoccupied.

Something was not right. Something was going on. He was sure the girl was at the center, somehow.

The subdued light from the ward filtered through the blinds as Jackson dug into the doctor's office files. He found his file but no file on the girl. His file said he was a paranoid schizophrenic and that he had had episodes before, in which, he thought he was an agent for a three-letter agency.

Confused and unsure of what to believe, he left the office and wandered the halls. Shaken, he went to the ac vent where he kept his notes. In the hiding place, he found only scrap paper, newspaper ads and menus from the cafeteria. *Was he awake or asleep? Were the missions real or delusions? What was really going on?* He stood looking at the wall, deep in thought, his eyes unfocused. Slowly he became aware of a mark scratched on the wall. *Ag ↓, Was that what it read?* A switch flipped. *Ag, the symbol for silver. Sylvie!*

The small arrow pointed down at the water cooler. He saw the panel screws on the cooler were slightly askew. He smiled, then walked away. *Later.*

That night he sneaked back to the water cooler. With a dime as a screwdriver, he removed the panel. Inside he found a note, which read, "*Ag JL 2L2R Ag.*" A clue but it made no sense to him. He put the note back, buttoned up the panel and returned to his room.

What could it mean? "*Ag JL 2L2R Ag.*" Ag he knew was Sylvie. JL was surely Jackson Lanski. But 2L2R, what was that? Thinking, he wandered the halls. He paid no attention to the direction. When he came to a corner, he might go left or right or straight. He just meandered. At a corner, he stopped abruptly. "Left, right, right left, two lefts, two rights, that's it!" He realized the words on the note were directions. He returned to the water cooler with Ag on the wall. Which way to start?

Facing the cooler, he turned left to the 2nd hallway then down to the 2nd right. The large red sign read, "Restricted Area Do Not Enter." Jack backed away and returned to his room. Later that night he returned to the restricted hallway. No one was in view. The door was not locked. He walked down the hallway, looking for some sign or clue. There. Above the door. "Ag." He looked in the window. *Bam.* Everything went black.

The attendant laughed, put him on the gurney and glided him back to the Clean Room.

Chapter 12: Jackson's Childhood

Jackson was a cowboy, in his heart, when he was a child. He had learned to ride and rope before he started school. His Grandma and Grandpa Muller had raised him on their small ranch, outside of Jasper. He had enjoyed growing up in the small Texas town.

He never knew much about his mother. Just the photo album his Grandma shared with him, telling him stories that brought her to life in his heart. She had died just after he was born, while his father was overseas, somewhere secret, a military adviser.

When his father retired from the military, they spent a lot of time together: Fishing in Toledo Bend and Sam Rayburn lakes, they brought home strings of catfish and bass. Hunting in the piney woods, they brought home deer, hogs, squirrels and turkeys. Jackson could take a deer at 200 yards with a neck shot. He aimed for the eye, when he shot squirrels. And in high school football, he was a tight end for three years. He joined the military right after graduation.

When he went in, they made him a sniper. He could make a kill at 1000 yards routinely. His longest confirmed kill was 1700 yards. He had heard stories of kills out to 3000, but he had taken those stories for what they were, stories. He was also an excellent shot with a pistol. Deadly accurate out to 100 yards.

At age 21 he had just come back from a tour in Iraq. He was contacted for a special mission. A terrorist cell that was located in New York City was planning an attack. The three members of the cell were going to hit a bookstore just off of Wall Street.

The store was a low security target and was close enough to destroy the exchange and many brokerage houses. Jackson was a sniper in the task force assigned to stop them. He killed three men that day.

He focused on these core memories to build the rest, out of the disjointed images floating through his consciousness. With strength born of desperation, he held on to them.

Chapter 13: Whiskey Tango Foxtrot

Jackson found himself roaming the halls of the Institute, groggy, without knowing how he got there. Dressed in hospital gown and robe, his feet in cloth slippers, he struggled for his memories.

He stood looking at the bulletin board. He realized, a note written in brown crayon, spoke out to him. It read, *Juno Lima Alpha Golf H2O 2L2R.* Juno Lima, that's JL that was him. Alpha Golf, AG, what was that? H2O. He remembered the water cooler. AG? Ag was the symbol for silver. Sylvie! He continued to roam the halls and eventually stopped to drink from the water cooler. Above was the scratched "*Ag* ↓". He saw the screws again. He finished his drink and shuffled away. His memories were slowly becoming clearer. Tonight he would come back.

That night he returned. He found the directions to Sylvie's room and followed them to her door. This time he made it into her room without getting caught.

In the room, was a curtain around her bed. He peeked in and found Sylvie lying unconscious. He checked her chart. She was heavily medicated with a series of unpronounceable drug cocktails. A drug induced coma, according to the chart, nothing else was wrong. They were keeping her sedated for what?

The clatter of footsteps in the hall, Jack quickly hid in the closet. The doctor and his assistant, Wissle, entered the room.

"How long do you want to keep her like this?" asked Wissle.

"Until, we get Lanski under control. He is becoming a threat to our plans for her."

"His father seems to have been effectively neutralized. But the two operatives have not reported back in, yet."

"Monitor Lanski, closely. He may have heard of his father's accident and try to go see him. And make sure he is kept away from Ms. Silverman." He caressed her shoulder absently as he spoke.

After they left the room, Jack was convinced they were responsible for his father's accident. He was determined to leave the Institute and take Sylvie with him.

Down the hall, Sylvie's orderly watched them leave, from the shadows.

The night security guard, as was his habit, was dozing comfortably in his chair. He had not seen Jackson enter or exit Sylvie's room. He did not see him, later, enter the pharmacy, where he switched Sylvie's medicine for placebos. Then, upon reflection, Jackson switched all of the anti-psychotic meds for placebos. "Tomorrow evening should do it,"

During the passing of the next day, the wards became progressively more chaotic as the patients came down off of their meds. With a lot of shouting, spinning, head banging and clothes rending, the different levels of crazy ran amuck. By the time that Jackson was ready, it was reaching a chaotic crescendo. The guards were all in the wards. No one was on the monitors. He made a beeline to Sylvie's room. She was lying in her bed, almost awake. Jackson said as he entered the room, "Hi, Sylvie. Do you know me? We have worked together. You are in danger."

Sylvie looked at him. "I'm not sure. What kind of danger? What is all the noise?"

"No time, now. I'll explain on the way. Here are some scrubs. Put them on."

"Where are we going?"

"We have to leave the Institute." He paused. He didn't have time to convince her. He changed tactics. "Look , I've come to help you escape and so you can complete your mission. It is dangerous here. We have to leave now."

They hurried through the chaos. The staff had their hands full with the crazies, no time left for patients who were not causing trouble. They went out the front door, unnoticed.

Jackson hot-wired a car. On the way to DC He explained that his father had been in an auto accident and was in the hospital. "I don't think it was an accident. I need to check on him."

Sylvie shook off the residual effects from the drugs. Her mind had cleared up considerably. She was at about 70%; that beat most people's 100%. At the hospital, still in her scrubs, she boldly walked into ICU and asked for the Lanski chart. The nurse looked at the chart on the closest bed, then moved over to the other bed and looked at the chart. "Here it is", she said. Sylvie studied the chart. She asked the nurse to get her some gauze dressings. When the nurse left, she switched the charts. She checked the vital signs monitor, shined a light into his eyes and told the nurse to change his dressings when she returned.

"Of course," huffed the nurse.

Jackson stood outside the door and waited for Sylvie's report. He could not have entered ICU without telling them he was the patient's son. He was not prepared to do that.

"How is he?" He asked as they walked away from the room.

"Not good. He has serious head trauma. Only time will tell. I have to go to the bathroom. Be right back."

In the Waiting room, he saw a picture of himself on the TV screen. He stopped to listen to the smiling woman with the heavy make-up.

"He may be going under many different aliases, including Senator Lanski's son Jack. If you see him do not try to apprehend him. Call the Institute at the number on the screen. Again, he is an escaped mental patient from the Institute. He suffers from Schizophrenia and may be dangerous. Do not approach or try to apprehend him. Call the number on the screen," she said, without ever losing her smile.

Jackson turned to Sylvie as she came back. Over her shoulder, he saw three men come up to the nurse's station. He heard one of them ask for the location of Senator Lanski. He stepped back out of sight as they approached ICU.

"Time to go. Now," he said. They headed out the back of ICU and through the Triage area out into the night. In ICU a vital signs monitor beeped a long continuous beep.

* * *

"Pull over and stop," she said. Jackson pulled the car over and stopped the car on a side street, not far from the hospital.

"We need to straighten this out. What the Hell is going on, here? What has your father got to do with my mission? Wait. What is the mission? We're in DC. My mission was in Tampa. Now we're being hunted. They said we were two escaped mental patients. What the Hell is going on?"

"I'm not sure about all of it. I lied about the mission part. We're not in a mission. But I can expl..."

"You lied about the frickin mission. Are you crazy?" She paused. "Silly question. Of course you are. It's all over the news."

"I can explain. I heard Doctor Einrich talking, he said they were keeping you heavily drugged. Do you know why they would do that?" he asked. "I think he caused my father's accident. I had to get out of there to check on my father; I brought you with me." He paused, once more. "Look, my memories are still scrambled, but, I think we are friends. I'm sure we worked together on your last mission."

"Did we complete the mission? Get the book? My memory has major gaps. What has happened since I got back? When did I get back?"

"I don't know. I have the same questions. We need a place to sort this out, to lay low for a few days."

Sylvie said, "I know a place we can stay."

* * *

The doctor smiled into the phone. "Her programming worked. She called from the hospital. She will take them to the safe house.

They will be gassed, shortly after they settled in there. Pick them up and bring them back to the Institute."

The doctor was pleased with success of his fail-safe. He knew she didn't even remember that she called him. It was a simple process, planted during her imprint. Now that it tested well, he would try it on other operatives.

"Did you take care of the Senator?" he asked.

"Yes, we caught up with him in the hospital. Both he and the driver are dead," said the voice on the phone. "Still haven't heard from the tails that were on them. Have you?"

"No, they haven't called or come back here, yet."

"I'll pick up Lanski and Silverman and bring them in," he said and hung up.

On the top floor of the Institute, in the doctor's pent-house apartment, Doctor Einrich hung up the phone. While he told himself, he didn't care about the trappings of wealth and power, he enjoyed the posh surroundings and sense of accomplishment they gave him.

The power was addicting. He wanted more. The Board was limiting him; he needed to shake lose their restraints.

To bring the imprint process to the next level, he would have to go after the power brokers themselves. Imprint them, one at a time, to do his will. He would control the strings of the marionettes that ran the world.

A chuckling giggle rolled up out of his throat. He quickly stifled it. It sounded just a tad too crazy to his ears. But still he smiled.

What was that? Was that a rat? He called Maintenance.

* * *

"Mr. Wissle, Where the hell is Dickerson? Isn't he supposed to be on the floor, now?" asked Doctor Einrich.

"I haven't seen him for a couple of hours. Yes, he is supposed to be on duty, now."

"Find him. His mother is coming over from the city and she'll want to see him."

Wissle went into the Security office. The guard was napping in the chair with his head back and mouth wide-open. Wissle took the soda can that sat on the desk and poured the contents into the guards open mouth. He woke sputtering and spitting out the cigarette butts from the earlier smoke break, totally against the no smoking policy.

"Get out of that chair." Wissle ordered. The guard jumped up and moved back out of the way. His gag reflex was almost under control. He ran to the men's room around the corner.

Wissle sat and looked at the monitors, checking for signs of Dickerson. Nothing. He rewound the monitor system and played the last two hours at high speed. There he was going in to Silverman's room. He slowed the speed of the tape. Dickerson came out of the room and approached the cleaning woman on her knees scrubbing the floor. She got up and they walked together to the utility closet.

A few minutes later she came out and went back to scrubbing the floor. Wissle waited. No Dickerson. He fast forwarded the tape. The cleaning woman came back with a gurney and put it in the closet. After a few minutes she left again. He waited. No sign of Dickerson. *Strange.*

Wissle went into the men's room. The guard was drying his mouth.

"Come with me."

"Yes, Boss."

The guard unlocked the utility closet door and stepped back so his boss could go in. Wissle entered and looked around. He saw the gurney between the shelves, then Dickerson in the corner, wrapped up in a sheet, asleep. Wissle kicked the nearly naked orderly.

"What the hell, Dickerson." Wissle kicked him again. "Get your ass up."

"Sorry, Boss. Can't." He held up his taped wrists from under the sheet.

"What the hell happened?" he asked. "Cut loose his wrists," he said to the guard. He yanked the sheet from Dickerson. "For God's sake. Where are your pants?" He threw the sheet back at him. "I'll be down the hall in Silverman's room when you get him dressed."

Lucy had left her bucket against the wall and entered the room when she heard the men coming down the hall. She and Jian got ready and waited just inside the door.

Chapter 14: Not Much of a Party

On her twenty-first birthday, Sylvie and her girlfriend, Lucy Wang, had gone out to a "trendy" club to celebrate. They spent the evening dancing and drinking. Sylvie had gotten a little tipsy. "It was her birthday, after all." At Sylvie's urging, they left the club early. She wasn't sure why, but she had to get out of there.

They caught a taxi. They gave their address to the Asian cab driver. Lucy and the driver exchanged glances. As they pulled away from the curb, two men exited the club and hurried to the van that pulled up. The van followed the taxi across town.

The cab driver said in Chinese. "We are being followed."

Lucy replied in the same language. "Yes, I see them. The van."

Sylvie lost the high and cheerful mood, instantly. She glanced out the back window.

"Let's find out what they want. Pull in to that alley."

"I don't think that is a good idea," said the driver in English.

"Nor do I," said Lucy. " I think we should just lose them and then head on home."

Sylvie's anxiety had returned. She was not sure why they wanted her, but she knew it was her, they wanted. She said, "Okay, let's go home." She would handle this by herself.

The taxi took the long way to their apartment. Looping around and occasionally back tracking, until, they finally lost sight of the tail. The taxi stopped. Sylvie and Lucy got out. Lucy said something to the driver. He nodded.

They unlocked and entered the apartment building. They both lived on the second floor.

Lucy said, "Sylvie, do you want me to spend the night?"

"No, I'm fine. You are just across the hall; if I need you. I'm not that drunk, for God's sake!"

Lucy smiled, said goodnight and entered her apartment. She walked over to a shaded window. In the alley below, the taxi was parked facing the street. Lights out, waiting.

Lucy made a sandwich and got a soda from the fridge. She turned off the light and sat down in a chair by the window over-looking the street. It was going to be a long night.

Across the hall, in her apartment, Sylvie was thinking about the events of the evening. Her friend and neighbor, had stepped out of character for a moment in the taxi. And the driver. He had acted like he was familiar with the two of them.

Why were those people in the van following her. She wanted answers. And she would not wait for the answers to come to her. She would go looking for them.

Sylvie, dressed in dark pants and sweater, gloves and sneakers, left her apartment through the back window. Down the drainpipe, into the alley, she followed her planned escape route. She had chosen this apartment because of the back exit.

In the alley below, quiet as a shadow, she circled the building, looking for anything out of the ordinary. In the side alley was a taxi, sitting with its lights off.

She approached from the rear. The driver was focused on the street view. He probably wouldn't have seen her if he had looked.

Sylvie had been trained to melt into the shadows and move without a sound by a master. She had been a gifted student.

Through the open window, her arm circled his throat in a submission choke. He passed out quickly from the lack of blood to the brain. When he came to, his hands were bound to the wheel and his feet tied to the brake pedal.

Sylvie sat in the back seat. She leaned forward, put his gun lightly against his temple and said. "We both can live through this if you answer my questions. Agreed?"

The driver nodded. "I'm on your side. I'm here to protect you."

"Why? Who sent you? Protect me from whom?"

"There are many groups that would like to use you as leverage against your parents," he paused. "Your father's family has had someone near you, since you were born. We have tried to stay close and unnoticed. It seems, I have failed to stay unnoticed."

"And what of my friend Lucy? Is she my friend or my body guard?"

"That is a question for Lucy. Would you please untie me? I can do little to protect you like this."

"It would appear that you could use a protector, yourself."

"Yes, so it would," he said somewhat abashed.

Sylvie untied him. "Are you here for the night?"

"Yes, I'll be right here."

Sylvie went back the way she came and up to the apartment. Inside she changed into pj's and a bathrobe. She walked across to Lucy's door and knocked. Lucy, startled by the unexpected noise, cautiously went to the door and asked, "Who is it?"

"It's me," said Sylvie. Lucy looked through the peephole and opened the door.

"Come in. I thought you would be asleep by now. What's up?"

Sylvie shut the door. She chose her words carefully. "How long have we known each other? Since college, right, and in all that time, you never felt you should inform me that you were some kind of bodyguard. Not the friend that you pretended to be. Think you can explain that to me?" Her eyes reflected the anger in her whispered voice. "Where's the trust we shared? It was all pretend? Do I even know you?"

Lucy sat and listened to her friend spew her anger.

"I'm sorry," she said. "I didn't wish to deceive you. I had no choice. I have been here to protect you."

"Protect me. I don't need protection. I can take care of myself, thank you very much." Sylvie paused. Things were starting to fall into place. "So you're not my friend, then who are you and who sent you? Who's the guy downstairs in the taxi?" She looked out the side window as she spoke.

"I was sent here by the Tang, the family of your father. You are always watched and protected. Your mother, too." She did not tell her anything more of her father. That was for him to do when he chose to. "Downstairs is my cousin, Yee Wang. Tonight, trouble is a foot. He will watch out for us. I suggest you get some sleep, while you can."

Sylvie gave her a scornful eye, walked out the door and into her apartment. She sat on her bed. The events of the evening played back in her mind. So her father was alive, she concluded. He was watching over her and her mother. Where was he? Why had he left? She lay down and tried to sleep, but the thoughts spun on. Finally, at about three in the morning she dozed off.

Downstairs, Yee the taxi driver, settled back and closed his eyes. It had been quiet; boring was good. He dozed. A garrote around his neck woke him. The mistake had proved fatal.

Lucy saw the shadows in the street below. She saw them pass the taxi unheeded; she knew Yee was no longer a deterrent. She hurried across the hall, quietly unlocked Sylvie's door and entered. In the dark, she made her way to Sylvie's bedroom.

A night-light cast a faint glow, enough for Lucy to take in the scene. Sylvie lay sleeping. The curtains blew in the breeze of the open window. Outside, the faint clink of metal shifting against metal. Sylvie woke. Lucy held a finger to her lips and pointed at the window.

Sylvie rose from the bed and stood beside the window. Lucy moved to the other side. A dark shadow stuck its head in. A knee sent him back out to crash on the ground below. A second shadow continued up the drainpipe. Behind him came a third. The second shadow dove into the bedroom. Sylvie engaged him. She threw a kick to his chest. It knocked him back. He countered with a punch which she blocked. They sparred back and forth in the faint glow. The third assailant entered in a long dive roll. Lucy took him on. She pulled a knife from a sheathe on the inside of her thigh and quickly dispatched him. The crash of the lamp and the banging of furniture signaled the end of Sylvie's foe; he kicked and squirmed, trying to dislodge the sleeper hold she had around his neck. She ignored his final tap-out on her arm as he slipped into unconsciousness.

The front door knob turned softly, as two more black shadows entered and came down the hall to the join the fray.

After them, a man in a gray suit entered with two more men in suits beside him. Inside the noise of the fighting was echoing through-out the apartment. The two girls were beating the crap out of the last two shadows.

"Just gas them, for God's sake. Let's get this done," he said to one of his men. The man walked to the bedroom door, tossed in a gas canister and shut the door. The noise stopped.

"Now we wait." In the distance, sirens could be heard. "We need to get out of here. Get our guys and the girl and let's go, now." The gas dissipated out the window, quickly.

The men tossed the dead men out the window to the ground below. They picked up the two remaining men and the girl and carried them downstairs. They put them in the van. Then they picked up the bodies and put them in the taxi, with the driver.

"Follow in the taxi. You'll ditch it down by the river," said the man in the gray suit.

"Boss, she took out three of our guys and was holding her own on the last two. That's five guys she handled. I'll tie her up, good."

"Yes, quite impressive," the boss said.

Sylvie watched from the shadows as they loaded the bodies. When the gas canister had come in the room, she dove out the window, grabbed the sill, swung on to the drainpipe and slid to the ground. A practiced maneuver that was part of her escape plan. There was no time to bring Lucy. She would have to watch for a chance to free her.

In the alley, the man started to get into the taxi. Sylvie bludgeoned him in the head and got in the cab. When the van pulled out she followed.

The dim dash-lights cast an eerie glow over the corpse in the seat beside her. In the back, the dead attackers, stacked like cord wood, bounced and moved to rhythm of the road, until the top man sat up and stared into the rear view mirror.

At that moment, Sylvie looked into mirror. She freaked. She nearly lost control of the cab. She swerved and the corpse slid back into the pile. She realized it was the bumpy road that was causing his movement.

Just as Sylvie had calmed herself, Yee's corpse took that opportunity to put his hand on her leg. She screeched. "Christ, I'll be glad when this death drive is over." and threw his hand back across the cab.

Outside the taxi, the dark of night was leaking away. Black of night was becoming gray. Beside the road the fields had turned to marsh. They had to be getting close to the dump site. Up ahead the brake lights came on.

In the pale gray light of early morning, Sylvie watched the driver get out of the van. He stretched and looked up at the sky. It was overcast. It would be raining before long. He waved at the taxi to come up. Sylvie waited.

The driver made an impatient gesture and started walking back toward her. He could not see her for the headlights in his eyes.

Lightning flashed and was followed quickly with a thunderous boom. The rain started to fall.

Sylvie turned on the wipers. She pushed on the gas pedal. The cab surged forward. The driver stopped, put his hand up to shield his eyes from the rain and tried to see if it was necessary to continue on back to the taxi.

He turned and started back to the van. Sylvie slammed into him. She broke his back with the hood of the cab. He bounced and slid in the mud to the back of the van. Sylvie stopped and jumped out of the cab.

She ran around to the side door of the van and threw it open. A single punch caught the groggy man in the head. He was out. A second man was lying in the van out cold. *No sign of Lucy or the man in the gray suit. They weren't there. But where?*

Sylvie loaded the three men into the taxi; she pushed Yee's foot on the gas pedal. The engine roared. Through the window she yanked the shifter in to drive. The tires spun as the cab lurched and launched in to the marshy pond. She watched the bubbles on the surface as Yee's taxi disappeared. The two men in the trunk ran out of air before they woke.

She climbed in to the van. It spun and side-slipped in the mud as she drove back down the two-rut road to the highway. Not the birthday celebration she had hoped for.

* * *

While Sylvie had been commandeering the taxi back at the apartment, the boss in the gray suit, had placed Lucy's unconsciousness body in his limo.

He had seen no need to dirty his hands with the disposal of the dead bodies. His minions could handle it. He took the girl to his office.

He would use her for leverage against the Tang. She should be coming around shortly. He needed her restrained before she woke. She was impressive.

In his office, he had a private one room efficiency that he used when he needed to stay in the city overnight. He carried her in and tied her to the bed and gagged her.

He still had three hours before Ms. Dickerson, his nurse/receptionist arrived. He shaved, showered, changed and readjusted his elaborate comb-over.

He didn't know he had the wrong girl. His ego did not allow for being wrong.

He had contracted with a rival Chinese Triad to deliver Sylvie to them. Their money and influence would help fund his research. He had big plans. Delivering Sylvie would go a long way to that end.

* * *

Sylvie parked the van in the alley by her apartment. She went up the drainpipe and into her bedroom. The soggy robe and pj's were discarded into pile.

Sylvie inspected her lean, muscled body in front of the mirror. Except for the bruises, nicks and scrapes, there was no serious damage. A hot shower and herbal ointment eased the soreness. Sleep would have helped, but there was no time.

She put on a dark running suit. Sylvie searched the shambles of the recent bedroom battlefield. Under the bed, was one sneaker. Behind the over-turned chest of drawers was the other.

In the living room, she filled her backpack with the things important to her: a family picture of Mom, Dad and Sylvie, a small bag with money, cards and her ID, a couple of yogurts and two water bottles. Not much, she needed to travel light and fast. She grabbed her computer.

Sylvie carried the backpack and laptop out the door and across the hall. Lucy's door was unlocked. She entered and locked the door, then setup the laptop on the table.

One of the benefits of a minor degree in computer science, her major was in music, was her close knit circle of hacker friends. Their server was a storehouse of apps for every occasion. She hacked into the DMV database.

The license tags had been pulled off of the van, but were inside the glove box. The van was registered to *The Institute,* with an address in Maryland. Nothing much showed up in the web search of The Institute.

It was a private sanitarium, run by a Dr. Einrich. It had been around about ten years. A web search on Dr. Einrich had given an office with a local address.

Sylvie pulled into the parking garage next to the office. The attendant recognized the van and waved her in. She entered the private entrance to the doctor's office.

A woman in a nurse's uniform sat behind a counter, strategically in the converging traffic patterns from both entrances. She looked up as Sylvie approached the desk.

"Yes?" she asked a bit snootily.

"Doctor Einrich," she returned, also snootily.

"Do you have an appointment?"

"I don't need one. Tell him Miss Silverman is here."

Ms. Dickerson was the quintessential gate keeper. She took her job quite seriously. The doctor was a very busy and important man. His time was not to be wasted. No one got by without an appointment, or confirmation.

She spoke into the phone. "There's a Miss Silverman here. She wishes to see you. What? Yes. Of course. I'll send her right in." Puzzled, she gestured to the door behind her. "You may go in."

Sylvie smiled at the nurse and walked around to the door, paused a moment to gather herself, and went in.

The doctor rose cautiously from the chair behind the desk. "Miss Silverman, How do you do?"

"Doctor, you have taken my friend. She is not who you think she is."

"And who do I think she is?"

"You think she is me, Sylvie Silverman. I am Sylvie Silverman."

That did not sit well with the doctor. "Have you some identification?"

"Of course," she said. She handed him the ID from her backpack. He checked it and handed it back.

"It would appear you are correct. Then who is this other girl?"

"She has nothing to do with this. She is Lucy, my friend from college. Where is she?"

"Why, she is in the next room, quite comfortable, I'm sure, but first let's talk." He was updating his plan as he spoke. "We can be of mutual benefit. I need your assistance on a project. Your friend Lucy is of no consequence; I will let her go after we conclude our negotiations," he said. "I have a project which is perfect for your particular skill set. It is exciting and sometimes even dangerous. We are involved in top-secret undercover activities."

The doctor was excited at the possibility of Sylvie being one of his operatives.

"I have some papers, I need you to sign." He opened the desk drawer. Took out a pen and reached across the desk-top to Sylvie. She leaned forward to take the pen. A mist came out the tip and caught her full in the face. She slumped on to the desk. The doctor chuckled.

He admired his own genius. He would send Lucy to the Triad and keep Sylvie for himself. She would be an asset to The Institute. With the imprint process, she would never know the decision was not her own. He would mold her into any shape that suited him. "Maybe, I'll make her my lover," he said.

He picked up her firm, tantalizing body. It felt so good against his stomach. He carried her into the bedroom. The girl on the bed would do. He undressed Sylvie and put her on the bed. As he removed Lucy's clothes, she started to awaken. He misted her with the pen. He stood and admired the two naked lovelies.

They were, indeed, prime examples of their species. Perhaps, he should make sure they had no anomalies. He examined them closely. He probed and prodded. He checked their breasts for firmness. He turned them over. Their buttocks were firm. The thighs well formed. He turned them over again. He rechecked the breasts. He compared the firmness. Sylvie in the left. Lucy in the right. Lucy's a bit larger. But Sylvie's were not undersized.

"I wonder if there is a taste difference," he said with a serious intensity. He ran his tongue around Lucy's nipple. "Um, salty." He did the same to Sylvie. "Huh, a hint of herbs and some kind of flower. She must have bathed, recently. Both are intriguing. A second sample is in order."

He wrapped his lips around a nipple. Suddenly, he spasmed. He went rigid, jerked and thrust. "This just won't do at all. Where is my scientific method?" He staggered, stiffly into the bathroom, jerking and thrusting. Thoughts of his mother's disapproval in his head.

* * *

Lucy caught bits of voices, then words. "Nah, they're still out. We should have some fun with them," said the man dressed in a white orderly uniform."

"We better get them to the Institute, first," the driver responded. "If we are late getting back they'll have our asses. Think of the long term fun we will have with them, then." He drove the ambulance on to the freeway heading to Maryland and the Institute.

Lucy lay listening to the men in the front of the ambulance. She checked for slack in the bindings on her wrists and ankles. She looked at the other passenger. It was Sylvie. That was good news and bad: Good that she was alive and no visible signs of injury; bad that she, too, was kidnapped.

She saw that Sylvie was, also, clothed in a hospital gown. Clothes, she'd deal with that after she got loose. She brought her legs up to her chest and through her arms and got her hands in front.

She took the super thin, two inch blade out of its hiding place in her hair, a small sheath above her right ear which her hair covered nicely. She cut the zip-tie from around her ankles and then cut Sylvie's bindings, before working on her wrist binding.

Lucy laid back. Sylvie was still out. Lucy needed to come up with a way to get them out of the ambulance. She looked around.

In a short compartment were spare uniform shirts and pants. She changed out of the gown and into the shirt. The lack of panties was troublesome, but low priority.

She put on the over-sized pants. The seams were a bit uncomfortable, but manageable. They were a loose fit, but hung on her hips, securely.

With the pant legs rolled up and the shirt tail tied together at the waist, she decided that was the best she could make of them.

The ambulance had rocked along the freeway during her change. A quick turn to the right bounced her into the cabinet with a bang. She jumped to the cot and covered herself with the sheet.

"What was that?" said the orderly. He slid the window back to look in. "I don't see nothing. Maybe you better stop and check it out.

"It is probably nothing. We're almost to the turn-off. We'll be at the Institute in five minutes from there. It can wait." Like most drivers he hated to stop once he had a full head of steam.

"Whatever." The orderly turned his attention to the radio. "You like Rap?"

Lucy waited for the music to start booming. She searched the drawers looking for weapons.

In the medicine drawer was hypos of sedatives and stimulants. She set aside hypos' of both. Scalpels were good. She looked at the Defribulater.

If she had enough time she could Macgyver up a Taser, but not in five minutes. The hypos and a couple of scalpels would have to do.

Lucy checked on Sylvie. Still out. She considered giving her a stimulant, but without knowing what had knocked her out, she felt it was just too dangerous. Better to wait and watch.

When the ambulance stopped at the exit on to the road to the Institute, Lucy opened the back door and stepped out, unobserved by the two head banging rappers in the front seat. She knew where they were going and she needed help.

The pimple-faced night worker, behind the counter, at the convenience store, happily gave her the change for the pay phone.

"This is Lucy Wang. Let me speak to Father Wang." When he came on she explained the events that had transpired over the last day and her desire to enter the Institute.

Father Wang said, "I will send your cousin Jian to help you."

"Please have him bring me clothes and shoes. And my weapons. Thank you, Father Wang."

Chapter 15: Deja Vu

Jackson Lanski awakened in the decompression ward. He recognized his surroundings with some anxiety. The support staff was attending him. His mission was a success.

The details... *The details? There were no details, Fading or otherwise. What was the mission? What the foxtrot had happened?* He lay there and searched through his recent memories, looking for the gaps. Determined to find what was missing.

Jackson walked out of his semi-private room and into the ward. He visited with the other patients of the Ward.

He grabbed a handful of peppermint candy from the Orderly station as he passed. Some patients were near catatonic. Some missions carried a heavy toll.

He slipped them a peppermint candy as he continued on around the ward.

He couldn't find the girl. He asked the attendant, "Where is the girl that is usually by the window." The attendant responded, "Which one?"

Funny, Jackson couldn't think of her name. He felt, he should know her name. "Never mind. My mistake," he said and turned away. Something was not right. Something was going on. He was sure the girl was at the center of it, somehow.

* * *

Jackson found himself roaming the halls of the Institute, groggy, without knowing how he got there.

Dressed in hospital gown and robe, his feet in cloth slippers, he struggled for his memories. He stood looking at the bulletin board. He realized, a note written in brown crayon, spoke out to him. It read, *Juno Lima Alpha Golf H2O 2L2R.. ...*

Chapter 16: Exotic Cuisine

A black Lincoln Navigator pulled into the alley beside NYC'S DELI. Two men in dark clothes got out. They stayed in the shadows as they made their way to the back door to the kitchen. The door opened to their knock.

On the counter where food was more often prepared, was a banquet of assault equipment. M16's, Glocks and assault jackets. Climbing gear, flashlights and radios. Gas masks, ski masks and gas canisters.

Colburn picked up an M16, removed, checked and reinserted the magazine, cycled the bolt, brought it up to the fire position and dry fired it with smooth precision. He, then methodically, checked the rest of the equipment.

Mr. Vincent said, "I don't normally get involved with the nitty-gritty in an operation, but this, I wanted to handle."

Senator Lanski watched Colburn check out the equipment. "Thank you. Do you think the Swat team will miss their stuff?" He said with a smile.

97

"Nah, this shipment never made it to them. It was lost in route. If you have to drop them, don't worry about it. They're clean; they won't trace back."

Colburn looked up. "Batteries?"

"Check the pocket of the battle vest. Should be in there," said one of the men.

Mr. Vincent said, "That's my nephew, Paolo. He calls himself Paul. Go figure. He was Special Forces." Paolo stepped up and shook hands with the Senator then Colburn. They appraised each other and nodded.

Paolo said, "This is Mario. He's good to go. Ex-cop, I trust him at my back, Senator."

"Call me Jack. If a four-man team can't do the job, more men won't help. We need in and out, quick and quiet. Do we have the non-lethal stuff? I would prefer to disable not kill."

"We have knockout gas, injection hypos and my favorite, the trusty blackjack," said Paolo.

"Colburn, anything you need, that you don't see?" asked Jack.

"No, I pretty much have everything I need."

Jack rolled out the plans of the Institute on to the counter. "Here's how I see it," he said, "but, give me your thoughts as they come up." He pointed at the plans. "The top floor is the doctor's private quarters. One floor down is his laboratory. The roof has cameras around the perimeter. We need to disable the one on the southwest corner. The skylights on the roof will give us access to his quarters. He doesn't have video cameras in there or in his office downstairs in the ward. Disable the security contacts on the skylight, then the security system at the keypad. You have thirty seconds to turn off the security from the time we breach the window." He paused.

"What about the doctor? Will he be there?"

"He might be. Use knock-out gas, before you enter." He continued, "We have a twofold mission: Get Jackson out of there and get as much information on The Institute as time allows. We need to be in and out of there quickly. The halls are monitored. We will have to take over the security station and monitor the staffs' movements. It should be lightly staffed, at this time of night. He tapped the security station on the plans.

"Mario, you will stay at the security station and keep us informed of their movements. Paul and I will find Jackson. Colburn will take out the front desk and, then, go after the info in the doctor's office."

* * *

The traffic from the shift change at the Institute had come and gone. The two black SUV's were parked on the forestry access road four hundred yards from the main building.

They made their way through the forest to the edge. A half-moon lit the hundred yards of open field that lay between them and their destination.

The Senator scoped the roof-top with his rifle. "There is the camera. Can you take it out from here, Colburn?" Colburn nodded and raised his rifle.

The "pfft" sound of the silenced bullet and then faint crash of it impacting the camera, did little to disturb the night. Inside the dozing guard didn't notice the monitor image turn to snow.

Shadows shimmered silently across the field. The team made it to the wall of the four story building.

Paul launched the grappling hook on to the roof parapet. He tested the rope, then quickly ascended.

He took ropes from his backpack, tied them off and dropped them over. The rest of the team climbed up. Once there, they regrouped and put on their gas masks.

Across the gravel roof, through the shadow of the AC condenser, they flitted with precision to the skylight. A soft glow emanated from the room below.

The Senator peered in the corner of skylight, a quick glance, then back.

On the other side, Colburn did the same. He signaled, thumbs-up. The Senator nodded and disabled the contact.

He cut the glass and opened the skylight. Colburn slid down the rope and was across the room silent as a cat. He disabled the security panel.

A growl came out of the bedroom. Colburn started nervously. Another growl, then it turned into a snore. Colburn relaxed.

He gave the all clear signal, put knock-out gas in the bedroom and shut the door. Again, the thumbs-up brought the rest of the team down the ropes.

Down the flight of stairs, into the laboratory and across to the elevator, once there, Paul and the Senator waited. Colburn and Mario took the stairwell to the ground floor.

They entered the security station without waking the guard and put him out for the night. He would sleep till morning, curled up in the corner. Mario took a seat and scanned the monitors. "Okay to move, Jack," he said as Colburn left the room.

At the front desk in the lobby, two guards were seated facing the front door, relaxed and inattentive.

The tink, tink, tink of the rolling canister, got their attention, a moment too late. They would sleep until shift change and have some explaining to do.

Colburn put the canister into his backpack. He walked into the doctor's office, opened the locked file cabinet, pulled out the Lanski file and then, radioed Jackson's room number to the Senator.

Jack and Paul rode the elevator to the wards on the second floor.

Paul said, "Senator, are you ready for this?"

"Call me Jack. Yes, I'm ready. I can carry my end."

They entered the ward. It was empty. Jackson's room was over past the orderly's station. Jack said, "Mario, what is the status? Any bogeys?"

"Yeah, we still have three orderlies in the break room playing cards. Just down the hall from where you are."

"Paul, go take care of them. Use the gas. I'll get Jackson." He took off his mask and entered the room.

Paul went to the break room and rolled in a canister. "Sweet dreams," he said.

Jackson lay awake on his bed, working on his memories. They were building back slowly on top of his core. "Remember, Damn it!"

* * *

He had dated Sylvie in college, after he got out of the military. They had enjoyed each other's company.

He spent a couple of holidays with her and her mother, Mandy, who liked him and saw him as a good prospective son-in-law.

Although, Sylvie and Jackson were more than friends, neither was ready to settle down. After graduation, their relationship took a sabbatical.

Her mother called him when Sylvie disappeared.

A mutual friend told him that she had been recruited by a government agency right after college.

When he had finally tracked Sylvie to The Institute, he applied for employment, thinking it was the best way to get to her. He remembered.

* * *

A man in a black battle rig entered the room. Jackson jumped up and then recognized his father when he lifted his mask. "Dad? Is that you?" He asked in a whisper. "They said you were dead."

"Yes, son. It's me. They tried. Can you travel?"

"Sure, I'm good to go."

"We need to hurry. Do you have any other clothes?"

"No, they took them, but there are some gray scrubs down the hall." They went to the staff locker room. He changed, then picked up a second set. "These are for Sylvie," he said. "We need to take her with us."

"We don't have the time or the room for more people. We have to go."

"Sorry Dad, but she has to come. I also, have some papers that I need to get. It won't take long."

"Son, we don't have time."

"If I go, she goes. I came here for her. I'll leave here, with her."

"Okay, son. Quickly."

* * *

The driver negotiated the ever present traffic back toward the restaurant in DC Chinatown. Mr. Wang sat in the back of the limo talking in Mandarin on the phone. "How is Ms. Silverman?"

"No change, Father Wang," said Sylvie's attendant. "She is still unconscious."

"Prepare her for immediate exit from the Institute. Time is short. We must be ready to move."

"Yes, Father Wang." He hung up and walked down the hall. The cleaning lady was mopping the floor.

He looked around to make sure they were alone and said, "Lucy, it is time. We must get ready to move Sylvie. Father Wang just called."

"I'll get the gurney and keep it in the cleaning closet," she said.

Lucy brought the gurney to the closet door, unlocked the door and entered. "Anybody home," she asked.

Huddled in the back corner behind the shelves was a nearly naked man with hands, feet and mouth taped. Fear radiated from his eyes.

"If you promise to be quiet, I'll remove the tape and give you a drink of water."

He nodded his head. Lucy pulled off the tape in one smooth yank.

"Ow," he said.

"Shh. You promised," she smiled and said. "Don't make me regret it." She gave him a drink. "What is your name?"

"Wyatt, Wyatt Dickerson. How long have I been in here? Can I leave, now? Food. Can I have some food?"

"My, so many questions, Wyatt. But let's see. Awhile. No. Shortly, if you behave."

"Could I have some aspirin, too? And a blanket?"

"Aren't we the needy person. Listen, if you do exactly as I say, you may live through this, but, screw up and you will die, painfully. Do you understand?"

He nodded with vigor. "Yes. Yes, I'll do whatever you say."

"Then stay quiet or I'll have to come back and kill you."

She threw a sheet over him. Then, brought in the gurney. Closed and locked the door. *It would be easier to kill him*, but she tried to keep killing to a minimum. "We'll see."

Wyatt lay in the corner. He adjusted the sheet over himself, as best he could with his hands and feet bound.

This was not unlike the punishment his mother used to give him when she caught him misbehaving.

She had been a hard-nosed Army nurse. Her idea of discipline was more attuned to a power crazed drill instructor than a mother.

Ms. Dickerson had gotten pregnant as a means to get out of the Army on a medical discharge.

She was never sure who the father was. When she went to work for the doctor, she fancied him to be the father, although, they had never had any sexual contact at all. Still it was her fantasy. She had used her influence to get him the job at The Institute.

Wyatt had a perverse sense of excitement at being in bondage again. *Perhaps the cleaning woman would spank him.*

Chapter 17: Sylvie Awakens

Sylvie and Jackson sat on the front porch, rocking, listening to the early morning sounds of birds and bugs, relaxed and waiting for day to begin. A favorite time of peace for them both.

The sunrise came to the forested hills; it changed the sky from pale blue to pink to yellow. Then the sun was up with a blinding flash of white that totally absorbed Sylvie's sight.

It faded to:

The morning sunlight lit up the pale yellow walls and the striped curtain, which went around her bed with a cheerful glow. She began to notice her surrounds and sighed. The alarms and lights signaled the support staff. Her orderly ran into the room.

"You're awake."

"Water," she croaked. "Where am I?" She managed after struggling to drink the water.

"We're in the Institute, but don't worry, Lucy and I are here to protect you."

"Oh, no. Where is Agent Lanski?"

"Who?" The orderly, Jian looked puzzled. "It'll all become clear, shortly."

Lucy rushed into the room. "Hurry, we must leave, now. They are on to us. Wissle is coming down the hall."

"Stay quiet, Sylvie." Jian and Lucy moved to either side of the door.

Outside the door, Wissle stopped and looked in at the sleeping patient. For the first time, that he knew of, her position had changed.

Curious, he entered, only to find a fist coming at his face. He barely ducked and took it on the top of the forehead. He staggered, but caught himself.

He was ready for the next blow and blocked it. He threw a punch in return. A kick from the other side caught him in the side of the knee.

He dropped to one knee and executed a three punch combo, followed by a leg sweep and got a moment's breathing room. He shouted, "Dickerson, Culp get in here, help!"

They came running. Culp first and Dickerson hopping after, trying to put on his other shoe as he came.

Culp had his Taser in hand as he entered the room. Lucy put a foot in his chest that knocked him against the bed. He dropped the Taser on to the bed. He re-entered the fray.

Four people, with obvious martial arts training, destroyed Sylvie's room. Chairs knocked over, tables crashed against the wall, bodies flew through the curtains.

The IV stand was used as a weapon. All in a blur of motion and shadows. The vital signs monitor went sailing across the room, as someone shoved it at their foe.

Dickerson looked on from the doorway. He cautiously moved in to the room. Working his way to Jian, he stayed back looking for an opportunity to taze him.

It came. Zap, Jian went down. He laid jerking and twitching. Lucy was alone, fighting Wissle and Culp.

Dickerson moved over and around the bed as he positioned himself with the Taser. He reached out to taze her. Zap, Dickerson went down. Now, he laid jerking and twitching. Sylvie had Culp's Taser in her hand.

Out of the corner of her eye, Lucy saw Dickerson go down. With a couple of moves and fakes, she set-up Culp and kicked him back to the bed where Sylvie waited and Zap he was down.

Lucy ducked as Wissle swung. They fought. And they fought. They matched punch for punch and kick for kick.

Slowly, Wissle's greater strength began to dominate. Lucy went down. Wissle, too quickly, moved to take advantage. He dove at her as she lay on her back. She caught him in the chest with both feet. Past her head, he met the wall with a loud crack. He was out of action.

Bruised and bloody, Lucy rose from the floor. She went to check Sylvie. "We have to leave. How are you feeling? Can you sit up?"

Sylvie sat up, but lay back down as she said, "Not too good. I'm weak as a kitten. I need a bit more time."

"I'll get a gurney." Lucy checked Jian on her way out. Nothing serious. He'd come out of it, shortly.

Jian regained use of his limbs. He dragged the bodies of the orderlies into the closet, stacked them like cord-wood. He checked Sylvie. She was back asleep.

Jackson and his father rushed into the Security Area to Sylvie's room. As they entered, Sylvie's orderly, Jian attacked.

He knocked Jackson back into the hallway with a kick to the chest. Then he swung a right hand.

Mr. Lanski blocked it and followed with a right of his own. They exchanged blows and blocks until Jackson recovered enough to rejoin the fray. While he fought with the orderly, his father plunged a hypo into the orderly's back and knocked him out.

Quickly, Jackson woke Sylvie. "Do you remember me?" he asked.

Sylvie was slow to respond. "I... I... don't know."

Jackson's father said, "We don't have time for this." He injected her with a sedative.

"Can you carry her?"

"Yes, I have her. We need to go to the doctor's office to get some files."

"Colburn is there. Tell him what you want." He handed Jackson the radio.

"Behind the couch is a busted seam. Inside are some files and a booklet. Get them," he told Colburn.

"Will do. How are you doing, Jackson? Good to hear you."

"You, too."

Jackson picked up Sylvie. With his father in the lead and Paul behind him, they left the Security Area and entered the ward, then on into the elevator.

On the first floor they met up with Mario and Colburn.

"Did you get the files and the booklet?" asked Jackson.

"Yes, I've got them."

Jackson's father asked Mario, "Did you erase the tapes?"

"Yes, and I left the tape out of the recorder. So, we won't be recorded as we leave."

"Let me carry her for you," said Paul. He handed Jackson a M16 and took the girl.

They went out the front door, through the parking lot, across the field and then back through the forest to the SUV's.

* * *

Lucy came running into the room. Jian lay unconscious on the floor. Sylvie was gone. Back in the hallway, Lucy ran toward the ward. Silent as a shadow, she followed the sign. She slipped through the passageway.

Dirty boot tracks. Down to the entrance and out into the night. The tracks led to the field. She ran on. The forest was still. Clink. Clink. Ahead the sound of man. She ran through the trees.

A car door closed. Another. Engines started up. She burst onto the forest road, in front of the SUV. She stood with her feet apart and her arms extended and her palms out. "Stop!"

The glare of the headlights swung around to reveal her in road.

Jackson said, "Wait. That's Lucy, Sylvie's friend from college. What's she doing here? Get her."

Paolo jumped out of the truck and covered her with his rifle. Jackson opened his door and stuck his head out. "Lucy, it's me, Jackson Lanski. We have Sylvie. Come on, get in. Hurry."

Lucy got in to the SUV and Jackson after her. She sat quietly, biding her time.

Sylvie lay back beside her. She checked Sylvie's pulse. Slow and steady. *Good.* On the other side of Sylvie sat Paolo. The four of them in the back seat made it tight. They had the doors covered.

Jackson looked at Lucy. "Quite a night. What are you doing out here?"

"I would ask you the same thing. Why have you abducted Sylvie?"

"We have rescued her, not kidnapped. Her mother asked me to find her."

Colburn sped the SUV down the forestry access road. Fast and efficient as an autocross driver, he sprayed dirt and mud from the tires as he handled the curves. Behind them the other SUV struggled to keep up.

Lucy needed answers and quickly. "How can I know you are telling the truth?"

"You know my father, don't you?"

"The Senator? Yes, I've seen him. He spoke at our graduation."

"You need to keep this to yourself. Can you?" The man in the front passenger seat removed his ski mask and turned around. "Turn on the inside light, Colburn," he said.

The full shine of the overhead light revealed a disheveled but recognizable Senator Lanski.

"Senator, what... I mean, Good evening, sir. May I ask what is going on?"

"My son called you Lucy. May I?" asked the Senator.

"Of course, sir."

"Lucy, we rescued my son who came to rescue Sylvie. He wouldn't leave without her."

Jackson rolled his eyes, but said "What are you doing here, Lucy?"

"I was captured with Sylvie when they broke into her apartment. They knocked us out with gas and brought us here." Some details, she thought, were not needed at this time.

"That is a bad place," she said. She hoped she had seen the last of The Institute.

113

Chapter 18: Senate Intelligence Committee

Senator Lanski entered the Senate Intelligence Committee meeting with a measured stride; he was met with looks of astonishment and disbelief. He ignored the hubbub, the questions and exclamations. The purposeful stride took him on up to the Chairman's side. Senator Lanski spoke in the Chairman's ear.

The Chairman nodded. "Senator Lanski has requested the floor for a matter of national security. The Senator has the floor for as long as it takes. And Senator, welcome back. It would appear that reports of your demise were premature."

"Thank you, Mr. Chairman. Yes, there was an unsuccessful attempt on my life by a rogue agency. One which I, and I suspect many of you, never knew existed. It is called *The Institute*. It goes under the guise of a sanitarium for wealthy neurotics. It is headed by a Doctor Einrich," The Senator paused to gather his thoughts.

"I discovered the existence of The Institute through my son. He had taken a job there, in the course of a case he was working on. After several weeks of no communications, I went to The Institute. Doctor Einrich told me that my son was a patient, who suffered from Schizophrenia and I could not see him or speak to him. I contacted the Deputy Director of the CIA, Jethro Kappland; we served in the military, together. I asked him to check into The Institute and Doctor Einrich," again he paused.

"While I was searching for information on this rogue agency, my driver noticed a car was tailing us. There was an accident, however, I believe it was no accident. I was not hurt, but two the men tailing us were injured and were taken to the hospital. Through a mix-up in route, they were believed to be me and my driver. They were attacked and murdered while in ICU. I thought it best to let the murders believe they were successful," the Senator stopped to let the story sink in.

"Will the Senator from Texas yield for a question?" asked Senator Laudermilch.

"Yes, I'll yield for a question from the senator from Rhode Island, without giving up the floor.?"

"If this is a risk to National Security, shouldn't it be handled by Homeland Security and not the Senate Intelligence Committee? We have plenty on our plate, at present, without this problem."

"No, this may be a problem of an inter-agency dispute, which is our jurisdiction, not Homeland Security's."

"Mr. Kappland is willing to testify before this committee. He will give us the information he has garnered. My son and his client have since escaped from The Institute and will testify before us. Mr. Chairman, I propose that we hold a Senate Investigation on The Institute, focusing on their activities, purpose, their leadership and associates."

* * *

In the Senator's apartment, Sylvie woke with a pounding headache. She looked around the large bedroom. Where was she? The furnishings were well appointed. Money. Who ever lived here, had money. She was wearing scrubs.

How had she gotten from the safe house to here? Where was Jackson? She jumped up from the bed and went to her knees as the pain fired off in her head. Slowly. She needed to go slowly.

Sylvie entered the bathroom. The beauty of Italian marble, Spanish tile and glass were wasted on her. She went blindly to the sink. Turned on the cold water, wet a wash-clothe and soothed her aching brow.

As the pain subsided, she noticed the large tub and next to it, the large glassed in shower. How long had it been since she had taken a long soothing bath. "I'll settle for a hot shower," she said to herself. But first she needed to find out where she was and who was she with. In the bedroom, Jackson called out, "Are you all right in there?"

"Getting there," she responded and walked back into the bedroom. "Nice place. Is this yours?"

"What? No. It's my father's. He put us up here. No one should look for us, here."

"How is your father? His chart showed some serious injuries," she asked. "How did we get here? The last thing I remember is going to the safe house." She thought for a moment.

"Wait. First I need a shower and a change of clothes. Any chance of that happening?"

"The shower, yes. The clothes, maybe. Hop in the shower and I'll look for the clothes. Any preferences?"

"A running suit or jeans and a top will be fine. Shoes would be a plus."

"I'll check."

Jackson looked in the closets. In one was an array of women's clothes. There was a lot he didn't know about his father's life. *Whose clothes? Well, no matter now*. He picked out a running suit and a pair of jeans and a tube top. She could choose. He grabbed a jacket, too.

In the shower, Sylvie was lathering her hair. Jackson had forgotten how nice her body looked. He caught himself staring and quickly put down the clothes and left the bathroom.

Sylvie said thanks and smiled to herself. Some of her memories were returning, too.

She came out dressed in the jeans and tube-top. Her hair wrapped in the towel.

"I feel much better. You should try it," she said. She gave a coy glance in his direction.

"Perhaps later. We need to contact your mom and let her know you're okay. Then we need to think about what we do next," he said and handed her a phone.

Sylvie looked at the phone with apprehension and did not take it.

"What's wrong?" asked Jackson.

"I don't know, but I'm afraid of that phone. You call her."

"Okay. I'll let her know you are alright." He called Mandy and gave her an update.

He told her, "I found Sylvie. I'm with her now. She will call later and check in, but she is in the middle of something, right now. Yes, she is okay. She'll call later. You're welcome."

He hung up. To Sylvie he asked, "What is it about the phone?"

"Just a feeling that I can't be trusted with one. I don't know for sure but back at the hospital, there was a sort of lost time or blank out that left me with a suspicion that someone had messed with my mind. I don't remember where I got the information about that safe-house. But they found us there and carried us back. So, no phones for me."

He nodded and changed the subject. "Was Lucy at the Institute with you?"

She looked up at him puzzled. "Not that I know of. I hadn't seen her since the attack at the apartment but the doctor said he had her in his office in town."

"Tell me about the attack. Do you know why they attacked you?"

Sylvie told him about the attack and her trip to the doctor's office.

Jackson thought about the situation they found themselves in. "They're not going to stop unless we stop them. But why you? We need to talk to Lucy and see what more she isn't telling us."

* * *

Josh Low was pissed. Mr. Wang sat across from him in the upstairs office of the restaurant. "Why am I only hearing of this now. That is my daughter. This doctor has got to pay for this."

"Sometimes, Nephew, I have to make decisions without checking with you. Yes, Sylvie is your daughter. She is quite capable. But she is in need of protection, and Lucy has been her friend since college. The two of them are a formidable pair. They took out five trained assassins in an attack at her apartment. Lucy is with Sylvie, now. Along with Jian."

"Who is behind the attack and abduction? Who has paid this doctor?"

"It could be a rival tong or even General Chong. We are checking all sources."

"Yes, the PLA could be involved. Thank you, Uncle. I'm sure you will let me know, soon," Josh said. He saw no benefit in pushing further. Something was amiss. He would send his own feelers out. Perhaps, things were not as they seemed.

* * *

Jackson Lanski woke in the decompression ward. Began to notice his surrounds and sighed. The mission was a success. The details faded as he lay there relaxing and decompressing. The Support staff attended him and closely monitored his progress.

Jackson walked out of his semi-private room and into the ward. He visited with the other patients of the ward. He grabbed a handful of peppermint candy from the orderly station as he passed. He slipped peppermint candy to them as he continued on around the ward.

At last, he saw the one he was looking for. She sat in a wheelchair by the window. She stared out the window. Slowly, Jackson felt the panic rise. "No it can't be. This wasn't right."

He was back at the Institute. "NO! NO!" He moaned. She looked up at him and said, "Wakeup. Wakeup. You're having a nightmare. Wakeup."

Jackson's reality shifted. Sylvie was shaking him. He was in bed at his father's condo.

"You were crying out in your sleep," she said. "Were you back in the Institute?"

"Yes, it was the same as if I had returned from a mission. I couldn't tell the difference. How can I be sure this is real? Will I wake up back in the ward again?" Sylvie cradled his head. "It's alright, I'm with you. It's real, I'm as sure as I can be."

Jackson fell asleep in her arms. Sylvie laid him back in the bed, got in beside him and wrapped her arms around him. He had tweaked her motherly instincts, but she couldn't deny the emotions were more than motherly and they were as strong as in college. He had come after her into The Institute, and now he was suffering, because of her.

* * *

Doctor Einrich sat in his office. Across from him stood Wissle, Culp and Dickerson. Wissle had a neck brace and multiple bruises and cuts. Culp looked much the same minus the neck brace.

"Men in black battle rigs broke in and abducted Silverman and Lanski? Where were you during all this?" asked the doctor.

Wissle replied, "I am afraid we were overcome by superior tactics, sir."

"What the hell are you telling me? You were found in Silverman's closet. Dickerson, no marks on you. Why not? What were you doing during this attack?"

"I was tied up in a utility closet, until Wissle and Culp untied me. I entered the room and with my Taser I disabled one attacker before I was rendered unconscious, sir."

"Wissle, you take these two and find Silverman and Lanski. Get them back here. They have the book. Bring them and the book to me."

"Yes, sir. I need to gather intel and put together the equipment. I'll take more men as well. I need to overpower them if you want them alive," said Wissle.

"Yes, I want them alive if possible."

Chapter 19: Senator and Mr. Vincent Again

At NYC'S DELI, Senator Lanski met once more with Mr. Vincent.

"Well, you were right about the hit, Senator. They would have taken you out at the hospital."

"So it would seem. My thanks for your help. The institute caper was a success. Thanks for the loan of your nephew and his partner. They did their jobs well."

"Paolo is a good boy. You need him again, just call."

"Thanks, I will. I need the second part of the plan to happen, soon."

"We're set to go, whenever you're ready."

The Senator grabbed his meatball sub, the reason he was here and said, "I owe you one, Mr. Vincent."

Outside of Washington DC, at a small airport, Jackson and Sylvie climbed aboard a Cessna four passenger airplane. They had little luggage, an overnight bag, a duffel bag and a briefcase. In the briefcase was the Russian booklet.

Jackson gave the duffel up to be loaded. Sylvie handed the overnight bag to the pilot. He loaded the bags into the small cargo compartment. Jackson kept the briefcase with him.

They took off and headed west towards the Blue Ridge Mountains. About two hours into the flight, the pilot radioed in that he was having engine trouble and needed directions to the nearest airport.

A person in Elkins, West Virginia, reported hearing a plane with engine trouble, fly kind of low over his house. "It was sputtering," he said. A farmer outside of Buckhannon, West Virginia, reported seeing a column of smoke coming up from a nearby wooded hillside.

The crash site started a small forest fire. By the time the fire was put out and the site was investigated, there was not much left to tell the tale. Twisted metal, melted aluminum, small pieces of bone and not much else.

The evening news lady came on with her usual plastic smile. "Four people died in a small plane crash in western West Virginia, near the town of Elkins. The pilot and three passengers went down apparently after having engine trouble. Among the passengers were the son of Senator Lanski of Texas, Jackson Lanski and his companion Sylvania Silverman. Senator Lanski, as you may recall, was mistakenly reported deceased, earlier this week, from injuries received in an auto accident. We're sorry for your loss, Senator."

Chapter 20: Dapper Gentlemen Again

In the paneled boardroom, the smell of money and expensive cigars waft through muted glow of the green shaded lamps, reflected in the hand rubbed wood of the tabletop. The dapper gentlemen sat around the long mahogany table.

The dignified group of self-assured men of understated wealth and power. The men behind *the men of power*, together once again to deal with the problems of The Institute.

The Jewish gentleman at the head of the table spoke without preamble. "The doctor has created a difficulty with his Institute. His plan was a bit optimistic, as it were. We had gotten along quite well with agents purchased from other agencies. Now, there is a threat of this Institute being linked to us. I propose we cut our losses and remove the doctor and his Institute."

He looked around the table. On his right the Spanish gentleman said, "And what of the book he was supposed to get? I fear it has evidence to implicate us in some significant assassinations."

Across the table the Asian gentleman spoke up, "It was destroyed in the plane crash with Mr. Lanski and Ms. Silverman."

"Are we sure of this?"

"Yes, we have the charred remains of the booklet."

"Are there copies?"

"It doesn't matter. Only the original would hold any weight. Copies are just another conspiracy theory."

"And the identities of the bodies, are they confirmed as well?"

"There was little left to identify, but DNA tests confirmed it," replied the Asian.

"Then it's over except for the doctor and his cohorts at the Institute. Am I right?" asked the Spaniard.

"I say we close this chapter and move on." The Jewish gentleman sat back in the chair at the head of the table. "I will take care of the disposal of the doctor and his Institute."

"And what of the doctor's technology? It is too dangerous to have in the hands of our enemies," said the Austrian.

"Yes, it must be destroyed, immediately. Agreed?" asked the Chairman. "Then, it shall be so. Is there anything further? Then we are adjourned."

They rose from the table. "Mr. Wang, would you join me for a brandy?" asked the gentleman at the head of the table. After the others had left, they retired to the study.

They each sat in wingback leather chairs facing a small tea table in front of the fireplace. A small fire was crackling cheerfully against the first chill of autumn. The leaves and the temperature were starting their perennial descent. The fire cast a warm glow on the room. An elderly manservant served the brandy from a side table next to the fireplace.

"Leave the bottle on the table. Thank you, that will be all for now. I'll ring if I need you," said Mr. Silverman.

He continued, "Mr. Wang, I suspect your Mister Low will be greatly saddened by the news."

"Yes, Mr. Silverman, he has gone to great lengths to protect his family."

"As do we all. I was not so fortunate. As you know I lost my wife to a car bomb attack. Though, my daughter and granddaughter are very precious to me, I have not seen or heard from them for over ten years. It is a sacrifice we are forced to share."

"Yes, choices have consequences."

"I know that Sylvania is your Mister Low's daughter, though, I thought it best to keep that information to myself."

"Yes, it would seem, that there is a connection to you as well. Your granddaughter, is she not."

"Yes, we have a mutual interest in her well-being. Can we work together on this?"

"We have been watching over her since, before your wife met her unfortunate fate. And we will continue to do so. Her and your daughter."

"I am indebted to you."

"No, it is our mission. We do not do it for you."

"Still, you have my support, if needed," Mr. Silverman relaxed back in his chair and enjoyed his brandy.

He thought of his daughter, Mandy. Memories of her like a *Super 8* movie, flickering scenes jumping through the years. *Here she is a toddler. Here she is a, sure of herself, eight years-old. Here she is at her coming out party. Here she is going off to college in her VW bug. Now pregnant with Sylvie. Her and little Sylvie.*

God, I miss them. Sylvie must be in her mid-twenties by now. That would make Mandy, at least, forty-something. Where has my life gone?

Mr. Wang looked at the dozing man and shook his head. Perhaps it's time for his retirement and the election of a new chairman. In the past, Mr. Silverman would never have dropped his guard in the presence of others.

On his way out, Mr. Wang told the manservant the status of his master.

* * *

Outside the Boardroom, was a curtained privacy nook. Senator Laudermilch had been waiting, hidden behind the curtains. The Austrian, Count Von Fuchs came out of the meeting, took out his cell phone and entered the nook.

"We must act quickly," he said. "The doctor's technology is much too valuable and dangerous for it to get out of our hands," said the Count. "And we must make sure that the doctor does not tell of our involvement."

"Yes, My Lord, perhaps we can take care of the doctor with the help of the FBI," said Senator Laudermilch. "I can contact the Assistant Director."

"Good, make sure we have our men in the assault team."

"Of course."

* * *

Mr. Wang said to his driver, "Take us by NYC'S DELI. I want a sub."

He called on the phone.

"NYC'S DELI, How can I help you?"

"Is the order for Vincent Wang ready?"

"Just a second, I'll check," he paused. "No, sir. It will be ready for pickup in thirty minutes."

"Thank you. I'll be there."

Vertical blue neon flashed and flickered *NYC'S DELI.* As the limo pulled up to the curb. The loading zone sign kept the space available for certain particular customers.

"Mr. Wang your order is ready. You can pick it up in the kitchen." The clerk behind the counter directed him to double swinging doors.

His driver opened the right hand door for Mr. Wang. The kitchen clamor of pots, pans and Italian voices came out with the smells of pizza, pasta and sausage subs. A cook looked up and pointed to the walk-in cooler, in back. They walked on back. A *tough* stood by the door. He held up his hand to stop the driver. Mr. Wang held opened his coat as he nodded to his driver. The *tough* opened the cooler door. Mr. Wang went in. Sitting on a crate of lettuce, was Mr. Vincent.

"Mr. Wang, how are you doing? How's your family?"

"Fine, we're fine. And you, how is your family?"

"We're fine. What can I do for you today?"

"I have learned that Senator Lanski has asked for a congressional investigation of The Institute and Doctor Einrich."

"Oh," said Mr. Vincent.

"Yes, and the committee has decided to cut their losses. The doctor has become a liability. They will eliminate him and The Institute. May I suggest, you remove your personnel."

"Thank you for the heads-up. I'll pull them out, immediately. Do you need any help with the trash disposal?"

"I think not. But, another committee member is handling it. We'll see."

Mr. Vincent adjusted his buttocks on the crate. "The Senator's son has a connection to your Mr. Low, right."

Mr. Wang said, "Yes, he and Ms. Silverman were assisted in their escape by the Senator and your nephew, Paolo. Is this not so?"

"It appears, that we both have been busy." Mr. Vincent paused. "The plane crash has been accepted as fact. They are believed dead. The false DNA results helped cinch the deal."

"Yes, my nephew was able to handle those tests," said Mr. Wang

" You have many nephews."

"As do you. A large family is indeed a blessing."

Mr. Wang picked up his order on the way out.

Chapter 21: FBI at The Institute

Doctor Einrich sat in his office. Across from him, again, stood Wissle.

Wissle said, "Did you see the news about the plane crash?"

"Lanski and Silverman's plane? Yes, I saw it. It is a bit too convenient," he said. "Is your team ready to go?"

"Yes, sir. We're ready."

"Good. Find out the truth and if they're alive, bring them and the book to me. Go, now."

As the three men drove out of the parking lot, a convoy of black SUV's with blacked out windows pulled in. Men in FBI battle gear and body armor jumped out. They spread out in military precision to cover all sides of the building and inside through the glass doors.

Wissle called the doctor. "Boss, the FBI is coming in full battle array. Better get out of there."

The doctor stood and began quickly to collect up papers and files. He put them in a briefcase just as the door opened.

"Doctor Einrich, please come with us," said the agent in charge. "I'll take that," he said as he took the briefcase from the doctor.

At the roadblock, Wissle and his crew were sitting in The Institute van, waiting to pass.

"FBI. Please get out of the van. Put your hands against the van. Spread your feet." The agent patted them down for weapons. "You have the right to remain silent..."

Chapter 22: Wissle Goes After Them

Wissle, Culp and Dickerson entered Doctor Einrich's in town office. The nurse looked up from her desk.

"So what have we here? Son, what brings you into town?"

Dickerson looked at Wissle. Wissle nodded.

Dickerson said, "The FBI has raided The Institute. They have taken the doctor in to custody. They may come here soon. They didn't have anything on us. Thought we were just orderlies."

"Mr. Wissle, what are your plans concerning the doctor?"

"I expect the doctor can take care of himself. He sent us to find out if the plane crash actually killed Silverman and Lanski. And to retrieve them and the book if the crash was faked."

"Okay, contact me when you find out. I'll check on the doctor." She glared at her son, "Have you been behaving yourself?"

"Yes, Mother."

"Wissle, you tell me if he doesn't. You hear?"

"Yes, ma'am." He knew it was best to go along with her. She was a power behind the scenes and she had the doctor's ear.

They drove the van to Wissle's rented storage space. Dickerson had not said a word, since leaving his mother's office. He sat in gloomy silence. Finally as they parked and got out, Dickerson said, "You wouldn't really tell my Mother would you?"

Wissle laughed. "Nah, I won't tell on you. But you better do what I say. Or I might." He couldn't resist twisting it just a bit.

Inside the space was Wissle's bug-out stash. Weapons, ammo, rations and other items he deemed necessary.

"Culp, grab a long gun and a pistol. Get ammo for each. You too, Dickerson."

He grabbed a tactical vest and battle rig, for himself. He handed battle rigs minus tactical vests to Culp and Dickerson.

Dickerson said, "Don't I get a vest?"

"Yeah," said Culp. "Me too."

"Sorry, I only got one." He had others but, they didn't need to know that. "We should be fine. Grab some rations from that box. Let's go."

* * *

"Hector this is Wissle. How soon can you get here?" He paused. "We have a situation. I need you here to help. Lanski and Silverman have left the reservation.

They have escaped and I need you to help bring them in. They have some serious man-power backing them." He listened then continued, "I'll expect you on tonight's flight, then."

After Hector hung up, he called Santo at his chop shop. "Hey, Cabron. How you hang'n?"

"Hey Hector. Waz'up?"

"I need couple of guns. You good to go?"

"Sorry I can't help my arm is still near useless. That girl sure worked it over."

"That's who we're going after. Her and her partner."

"I sure would like to get square with her. I got a guy here that owes her some payback. That Russian guy she stole the book from. You want him?"

"Is he any good?"

"Story has it, he's KGB. If so he hides it well. But he is another body."

"Okay, I'll pick him up."

Wissle picked them up at the airport. He was not all that impressed with the appearance of Boris, the Russian, and said so.

Boris said, "Is best to be thought less of," as he got in the back seat. Wissle looked at Hector who shrugged and got in the front seat. Wissle rolled his eyes to the heavens, then he got in and drove off.

"Do we have enough men?"

"I called in five more guards from the Institute. They are all ex-military and unhappy that their cush' job was in the tank. I explained who was responsible. That gives us ten on the ground." He pulled into the storage building parking lot. "The intel has them in the mountains near Luray. That's near the West Virginia border. We'll fly into Luray and proceed on the ground to their location."

Chapter 23: In the Cabin in the Woods

In the cabin, in the mountains near Luray, two men and two women sat around a roughhewn pine-plank table eating, a sort of, chicken stew.

"This is not bad for freeze-dried. Not bad at all," said Jackson.

Sylvie cast a glance at him. "If this is all that, then I should be able to wow you, when I cook," she said with a laugh. "This is almost edible. What do you say, Lucy?"

"Maybe with some five spice powder, it would be okay, that and soy sauce," she said.

Jian just shrugged his shoulders and kept eating. He'd had worse. And less.

"How long before they find us?" He asked as he set down his bowl. "This mountain air is starting to unclog my lungs. I'll need a tobacco transfusion when I go back down if they don't come soon."

Jackson said, "I could stay up here. I like it just fine. I'll go hunting tomorrow and get some fresh meat."

Sylvie looked across the table at Jackson. "The gunshot would be heard for miles. We can live on this freeze-dried canned crap."

"I found a crossbow and bolts in good condition over the cabinet. I should be able to take something with it, quietly."

Before the sun came up, Jackson was in the woods. Down the mountain and about a half mile away, he sat watching a stream meander through a clearing. The night became gray as the sun worked its way to sunrise. He hadn't moved, not even to scratch, for over an hour. He didn't think about the automatic hunting mode. As a sniper he had sat unmoving for several hours at a time.

The wild flowers perked up as the first rays of sunrise hit the clearing. He became alert to the smell of musk drifting on the faint breeze.

Across the stream, in that clump of small trees, he could see part of a face. Yes, there were the antlers. He waited. The morning birds fluttered down to drink.

The deer took a step and paused. Then another. He stood very still. Satisfied, he made his way to the bank of the stream and paused once more.

He dropped his head to drink. Jackson brought up his crossbow. The deer lifted his head. Ears up and alert. He looked back down the mountain. Jackson held his shot. Something had alerted the deer.

The deer went back to drinking. It sensed no immediate danger from downwind. Jackson sighted in on a heart shot and gently squeezed the trigger. The bolt caught the deer just behind the shoulder straight through the lungs and heart. The deer kicked its back feet out and bolted into the brush. Jackson never moved. After ten yards the deer stopped and looked back. He slowly sank to the ground and rolled over on his side. Jackson waited.

The Sun was up and sent a glowing warmth up the side of the mountain. Jackson skinned and gutted the deer. He put the backstrap and hams in his game bag and buried the rest. He knew the varmints would dig the remains back up, but for now, the evidence of his presence was hidden. He crept back to the cabin, focused on the sounds of the forest.

Jackson approached the cabin. Jian signaled him from the stand of trees by the woodshed. With the meat over his shoulder, he opened the cabin door.

"Home the hunter. Home from the hill," said Sylvie. She smiled and came over to take the game bag.

"It's too heavy. I'll put on the counter." He took it to the kitchen side of the room.

"What did you get? A moose? Too heavy. I'm such a faint hearted girl."

Jackson smiled back. "I know better. I had it handled, that's all." His face became serious. "We have guests on the mountain. We can, probably, expect them around dark."

Sylvie didn't need to know how he knew. Jackson was in his element. She nodded her head. She took the meat and put it in the meat locker.

Jackson turned to Lucy. "Would you relieve Jian, for a while? Thanks."

Jian came in. "Lucy said that we had guests," he said.

"Yes, I'll go down and reconnoiter. I know you are not used to being in the woods. Where would you be at your best? How do you want to position yourself?"

"I'm good, no problem. I've had wilderness training. I'll setup over by the woodshed. It has good shooting lanes and easy access back to the cabin."

"Can you shoot a crossbow?"

"No, but I am good with this." He held up a K-bar combat knife. Then threw it and stuck it in a post at the far end of the cabin.

"Good, we'll need some silent kills to start with. I'm going to set some traps, out there. So you'll need to stay close to the cabin." He sat and thought. "Sylvie, what about you and Lucy? How do you want to play this?"

"If you set your traps on the sides of the perimeter and leave the front approach clear, we can move in and out that way as needed. They will expect us to cover the front."

"Yes, they will put a shooter on the front door and wait for shots of opportunity."

Jackson went over to the gun cabinet. He took out a model 77, with a 500 Leupold scope, in 308 caliber and a box of ammunition. Twenty rounds he hoped it would be enough.

"We don't have a lot of ammunition, so we need to kill other ways first."

Sylvie, if you and Lucy stay inside and let the fight come to you, you will be at an advantage in the dark and in close quarters. If as you fight, you retreat upstairs, it will give you the high ground and it will allow Jian and me to come in and hit from the rear."

"Sounds like a plan," said Sylvie.

"I'm going out, now, to take some of them, as they make their way up the mountain. I'll be back before they hit here."

"Take care of yourself. I just got you back. I'm not ready to lose you again."

"Yes, we all need to be careful. Jian, keep your eyes peeled. I'll tell Lucy the plan on my way past her." Pure business. Jackson would not let any thoughts distract him from his mission.

He stopped with Lucy and told her the plan. He cautioned her to be careful. But, he knew the words were wasted. She and Jian would do what was necessary to protect Sylvie. It was their primary mission. She smiled and nodded. "No sweat. Should be fun."

* * *

Jackson and his father had come to Jethro's cabin many times. The three of them had hunted these woods during his mid to late teen years.

After Jackson, returned from the military, he had spent some quiet time up here alone, recuperating and relaxing, before he jumped back into life, college and whatever else, awaited him.

Jackson had scouted the mountainside every day for the last week. He knew the terrain well. The most likely routes they would take and the best places for ambushes.

Around his waist he had a fanny pack with rope and other climbing gear. He carried the 308 strapped across his back and the crossbow in his hand loaded and ready. He had six bolts which he planned to plant in the bodies of six combatants.

* * *

At their base camp, Wissle and his crew were sitting around like a rowdy group of hunters. No sentries. No worries. They were the baddest bunch in the forest. They had dragged logs into a circle around the unnecessarily large fire.

"I'm ready for another beer," said one and walked over to the SUV. He opened the back and got a can out of the cooler.

"I'd leave that alone if I was you, Drexle. I don't need a drunk idiot with a gun up there in the dark," said Wissle.

Drexle turned and glared at Wissle. "I didn't know my mother came on this mission. How bout I do what I want."

Wissle remained seated quietly on the log. He said, "Now I can admire that in a man." He pulled out his silenced pistol and shot the man with three quick shots in the chest. "Deciding when he should die, like that. Anyone else need a beer?" A chorus of negatives came from the group.

In one of the SUV's, Boris watched the scene unfold before him. He became steadily convinced that this was a bad idea. These guys were supposed to be pros, but they acted, more and more, less likely to succeed. He needed to leave and leave now.

Wissle smiled at the group. "Now, isn't that quieter. Hector, go get the Russian. It appears we have an opening."

"Yes, Boss." He hurried over to the SUV. "The boss wants you." He opened the door.

Boris was reluctant to get out. "But, wait. I..."

Hector took his arm and helped him out of the vehicle and over to Wissle.

Wissle said, "You need to come up the mountain with us." Then to the others, he said, "They are up there about a mile and a half from here. We will make our way there and surround the cabin just at dark. We will surprise them and either capture or kill them.

Boris said, "I not so young. I should stay here."

"If you stay, you'll stay right beside gerbil dick, there," said Wissle, pointing at the dead body."

"I try my best. But, will hold you up."

143

"I suggest you keep up. If you didn't read Russian you wouldn't be here."

"What, you know book? Is where?" asked Boris.

"Up the mountain," Wissle responded. "Time to mount up. Let's go."

Jackson watched the group of heavily armed men start to ascend. He moved off of the over-hang and ran fast and silent to the first ambush site.

As they came around a bend in the trail, they were forced to travel in a single file. The last man was out of sight for a moment in the bend. Jackson garroted him with the same rope he had hung up the deer to skin and gut. He slipped back in the forest.

The next to the last man continued another fifty yards up the winding trail before missing his comrade. He turned around, walked back a ways and quietly called his name. "Johnson where'd you go?" He turned back to the group. "Hey, guys, Johnson has disappeared. Hey, guys."

They were up the trail out of sight. He was afraid to speak too loud. Perhaps, he should have chanced it. He looked down at the arrowhead that suddenly appeared sticking out of his chest. Surprised, he just stood for a moment, then collapsed to the ground, dead.

Dickerson turned to say something to the guy behind him. He wasn't there. No sign. Dickerson hurried to catch up to the other men in the file. With furtive looks over his shoulder, he scrambled on past until he came to Wissle. "Boss, the last two guys are missing."

"Missing, what do you mean, missing?"

"I don't know. They're just gone. I turned to say something and they were gone."

"They'll catch up, or they won't. We don't need them. We have plenty of fire power, enough to take Silverman and Lanski."

"You think they are alone?"

"Who could be with them?"

Dickerson wasn't so sure, but didn't say so. Wissle was in no mood to hear opposing views. Dickerson hoped it would not bite them in the proverbial posterior. But he continued to walk behind Wissle, not willing to be the last guy in the file.

In the file was: first Wissle, then Dickerson, Boris, Hector, Culp and the two remaining guards from the Institute. Each man heavily armed with rifles, hand guns and gas and percussion grenades. Wissle and Hector, each had their own tactical vests or flak jackets. The rest did not.

Jackson watched them move up the trail. He scrambled through the woods. But the need for speed was over-ridden by the need for quiet. So, he didn't reach the bottleneck before they did.

That left him with two choices: He could wait and follow them through the bottleneck. But, they would have a clear view of their back trail and him on it. Or, he could take the more difficult, but faster route up the cliff face, unseen and get back ahead of them.

It was a narrow trail with switchbacks and some places just had footholds cut into the rock wall. His godfather, Jethro had shown him the route several years ago.

Jackson didn't hesitate and took the faint trail to the cliff. The trees and brush fell away and suddenly, he was looking out over the forest tops in the valley 500 feet below.

The trail lead onto a narrow ledge covered with loose rocks, bird droppings and twigs. Carefully, he picked his way over the debris.

He made it to the first switchback. Then the second. Halfway up the third trail, the ledge had a three foot gap in the trail. There were hand-holds cut into the cliff wall above the gap.

Jackson had used them crossing the gap in the past, however, this time, there was what appeared to be a large bird's nest right on the other side of the gap. It looked like there was no room for him to step next to the nest. Jackson stood on the edge of the gap.

He slipped the rope through a carabineer on a cam from his fanny pack and tied it around his waist. With his left hand, he grabbed the first hand-hold. He reached his right hand to the next hand-hold.

He secured the cam in a crack in the cliff-face, above and as far to the right as he could reach.

With his foot still on the ledge, he tested the line. It felt solid. Time was against him. He swung out and over the gap and the nest. Inside the nest were eggs. He needed to get out of there before the parents came back.

He landed on the ledge past the nest, pulled the rope through the carabineer and made his way up the ledge to the next switchback. He hoped his luck held out. Those could have been an eagle's eggs.

Eagles could be deadly with him exposed on a ledge like this. The advantage was all theirs.

From high overhead came the screech he dreaded. He saw the eagle. He bolted up the trail. Just one more switchback and he would be at the top and in to the trees.

The ledge opened a little wider. He lost sight of the eagle. He made the switchback. Up on the next ledge, he set another cam and carabineer and secured his rope. *Where was that eagle?*

The outraged parent attacked the interloper on the ledge. Jackson covered head with his arms and ducked down to a squat as the eagle swooped down.

The eagle came close enough for Jackson to be buffeted by the wind of the wings in passing. Just missing him with the sharp talons of the big bird of prey.

Jackson ran up the ledge trying to get to the trees before the bird came back. He had fifty feet of rope and at least a hundred feet to go to the trees.

He was at the end of his rope, when the eagle dove once more. He reset his rope and gear.

The eagle slammed into him with enough force to knock him head first into the cliff wall. He bounced off and only the rope saved him from going over. Jackson was out cold.

The eagle did not come out unscathed, either. It wobbled to the edge and glided down to its nest.

* * *

Back at Wissle's base camp, the glow of the burning embers cast a pattern of shadows around the site.

In one patch of light lay the body of Drexle, the man Wissle had shot. He jerked to a sitting position, put his hand to his chest and grimaced in pain. He opened his jacket to reveal a tactical vest with three slugs flattened in a tight group.

He put the slugs in his pocket and then staggered over to the SUV and got a beer. "With your permission, Mr. Wissle," he said as he took a chug of beer. "I'll give those slugs back to you, soon," he said with a laugh.

He grabbed a six-pack and put the beers in various pockets in his battle rig. "Time to go save the day."

He headed up the trail. He took out his flashlight. "God, they leave a trail a woman could follow." He threw the empty beer can in the bushes and got out another one.

He thought alcohol and gunpowder, was a wonderful combination. One, he richly enjoyed.

* * *

Sylvie looked out the western window. "The sun is going down. It'll be dark in just a few minutes. I wish Jackson was back."

Lucy said, "I'm sure, he'll be back in time. I'll check on Jian."

She went to the eastern window over the kitchen sink. She opened it and made the call of a Beijing Warbler. Jian answered from the other side of the woodshed.

"He's good. Nothing, yet."

Sylvie and Lucy had their weapons set up in three locations. Near the front and back doors and upstairs on the loft hallway. They had checked them over and again.

Most of the furniture was cleared from the main rooms. That which remained was placed so that the attackers who used it for shelter would be in a crossfire from the sides of the loft.

Sylvie mounted a shotgun between the loft railing spindles, straight at the front door, with a cord for a trigger pull. Two cords ran, one to each side of the loft. A woman on either side could use it.

Outside the call of the Beijing Warbler sounded its warning. Things were about to start.

Jian watched as the shadows moved through the woods to the flank of the cabin. One stood behind the woodshed and in front of the stand of trees Jian was in. He waited for the others to get settled. He had three attackers located by the noise of their movements.

Silent as the shadow moving in starlight Jian slipped up behind the shadow by the woodshed. With an arm around his throat, he stabbed him between the ribs and up into the heart with a twist of the knife. The man was dead before he made a sound.

Jian eased him slowly to the ground. He collected the dead man's weapons and went back to the stand of trees.

Jian went after the second man. As he approached from behind, the man unexpectedly, dropped down to the prone position and brought his rifle to bear on the cabin.

Jian waited. A loud crash and scream cut off sharply, signaled the success of a sprung trap. Two down, now, how many more?

"Wha... What was that?" said Dickerson.

"Be careful. There are traps." Wissle told Dickerson to cover the front porch.

"Hector, you and the Russian cover the left flank. I'll go in through the back door."

"Where's Culp?"

"On the right flank with the other two," said Wissle. "Watch your lines of fire. Keep the cabin between you and them. When the flash bang goes off, charge the cabin and move to the window and back door. Wissle went around the left side of the cabin, the opposite side from where Jian was stationed. Jackson was supposed to cover that side.

* * *

Jackson woke on the ledge. He was not sure where he was or what had happened. *Was he on a mission?* He slowly cleared his head. He had a rope around his waist. The eagle, what a trip. He had just got his butt kicked by an eagle. Careful of the ledge.

He looked at the starry sky. He had been out for an hour. They were at the cabin by now. He had to go, now. No time for careful. He wound up the rope and burst up the trail into the woods. *They can hold them off for ten minutes. They have too.*

* * *

As soon as Hector got in to position, he whispered, "Boris, Boris." But, Boris was gone.

He was sure that this was not going to turn out well for Wissle and Hector.

The light of the quarter moon was enough for the man from Russia to navigate back down the way he came up. He cautiously made his way down the trail.

A voice out of the dark said, "Who are you? What are you doing here?"

"Please, no kill me. They make me come. I look for book. Is all."

"You're the Russian. I thought you were dead."

"Nyet. I get that a lot. No dead. Please, I go down."

"You should try to find Senator Lanski. Tell him about the book. You can trust him. He's my father."

"Senator Lanski. Dah. Goodbye."

Jackson hurried off again at a hard run. Boris breathed a sigh of relief and continued down the trail. Soon, he thought he would be at the SUV and out of here.

Boris heard the singing, well before he came up on the fool, Drexle. He hid, off the trail, until the man had passed. He hurried on down the path.

That man had been shot. He shook his head. Well, Boris, himself, was evidence that things were not always as they seemed.

* * *

Culp was laying prone waiting for the flash-bang. They were supposed to rush the cabin after the flash-bang. In the cabin, the women were waiting. Sylvie was posted at the front door. Lucy at the back. They had seen no one.

Sylvie said, "Up the stairs, quick."

The window on the west side crashed in. A grenade bounced across the floor. The women dove for the stairs.

They were up the stairs and on the loft floor as the flash-bang went off. They lay dazed but hidden when the doors burst open.

Dickerson came in the front and Wissle came in the back, followed by Hector. Culp was running toward the front porch. Jian caught him in the back with a thrown K-bar. He sank to the ground.

Wissle checked the downstairs. He ran up the stairs. When he saw the two ladies, he said, "Where's Lanski?" To Lucy he said, "What the hell are you doing here? You're the cleaning lady. For God's sake."

Dickerson came up the stairs. "The cleaning lady? Well. Well. It all comes around." He grabbed her and zip tied her hands quickly. "Fun time." He grabbed her breast and squeezed it. "This is going to be fun." Lucy seemed too remained groggy.

Wissle zip tied Sylvie's hands while she was also, dazed and confused. Hector waited by the front door, standing watch. He said, "Lanski is around here somewhere. We need to be ready for him. Dickerson, you will have time, later for Slap and Tickle."

Lucy looked up at Dickerson. "I knew I should have killed you. No good deed goes unpunished."

"Your English is real good, now. What happened to the pidgin English?"

Lucy smiled. "I lived in the US all my life. I'm fifth generation American. My family has been here longer than yours. Oh, and by the way, you're dead."

"What? What do you mean? How do you figure? You're going to kill me?"

"Oh, I'm not. Sylvie is." He spun around to face Sylvie. Lucy took the opportunity to swing a round house kick to his head. Right where it meets the neck. He flew over the railing and down to the floor below. He hit head first. He didn't move again.

"I lied," she said.

Wissle hit her in the side of the head with the butt of his gun. She went down. He turned and grabbed Sylvie. He brought her down the stairs. "Sit." He indicated the couch. She sat.

The back door opened. Wissle turned to see who it was. Jian stood there with his gun covering Wissle and Hector. "Drop the guns."

"Not going to happen," Wissle dropped behind the couch with Sylvie sitting on it. Jian shot Hector in the chest. He went down. Wissle shot at Jian; the impact spun him around and into the door, slamming it shut. His body lay against it not moving.

Wissle went over to Hector. "You going to be alright?"

He opened his vest and rubbed his chest. "God, that hurts. Yeah. Remind me to send a note to the manufacturer." He went back to check the body at the back door. "He's dead."

He checked Dickerson. "Dickerson's dead, too. His mom's gonna be pissed."

"Life is tough," said Wissle.

He knelt in front of Sylvie. "This ordeal is almost over. We will have you back at the Institute, shortly. Where is Agent Lanski? We need to bring him back with us."

"I haven't seen him."

"Oh, come now. We know this is his cabin. And that you came here together."

"Really, I haven't seen him, since around noon. He went out into the woods and hasn't been back."

"Well. I wouldn't have thought him the type to desert you."

* * *

Jackson climbed the chestnut oak behind the cabin. He made his way quietly across the cedar roof to the dormer window over the loft. He made the sound of the Warbler and waited. No response. Below Sylvie heard the signal. Started to talk a little too loudly.

"What makes you think I want to go back to the Institute? I'm through with that place. They are not on my Christmas list anymore." She rambled on, covering any noise of Jackson's approach.

Jackson worked the window sash slowly up, until he slipped through and on to the bed below. No springs to squeak. The frame was made from local saplings and strung with a rope web to hold the mattress. It was comfortable and quiet.

He removed his boots and stepped off of the bed. The door to the loft hallway was open. He listened to Sylvie.

"Wissle, you and Hector have a lot of explaining to do. With Jian and Dickerson dead. You two, alone, will face the authorities." Jackson smiled. Wissle and Hector were alone. Hector was with Wissle. *Good Girl.* She had given the information he needed.

"What are you going on about? The authorities will never know about us."

"We'll see." She continued to distract Wissle. "How many men did it take to capture a couple of girls?" She smirked at Wissle, trying to goad him.

Hector stood with his jacket opened, revealing the Vest underneath. He looked up at the loft railing just as the crossbow bolt flew through the air and struck him in the throat. It pierced his larynx and lodged in his spine.

He fell to the floor gasping and gargling out his last breaths. Jackson jumped back into the bedroom.

Wissle had been focused on Sylvie. He spun around toward the twang of the bow string and then back to the sounds of Hector dying. "What the hell?" Wissle peered up at the unlit loft. "That you, Lanski? I got your girl Silverman. Come on out."

Jackson stepped out of the room. He had a silenced semi auto pistol in his right hand. "You're all alone up here, Wissle. The rest of your men are dead." He came down the stairs. He wanted to get closer to Wissle. He moved to his left. He worked to get Sylvie out of the line of fire.

"Stop where you are. Lanski." He pulled Sylvie up in front of him.

"Not much of a shield. She's only five four and you're what Six-one or two. You can't get all of you behind her. Give it up. I've got a clear shot at your left shoulder."

Wissle quickly, moved right. Jackson shot him in the right shoulder. The bullet knocked him away from Sylvie and to the floor.

Jackson cut the zip tie from her wrists. "Are you all right?" She nodded and hugged his neck. "Took you long enough," she said.

"Well, ain't that sweet?" said a voice outside the door as he threw in a gas canister. "Soon you won't remember any of this." Drexle laughed. He waited before he entered the front door of the cabin.

Jackson untangled from Sylvie's hug, but too late. Already the gas had him. He and Sylvie went down in a pile. The last sound they heard was a loud bang.

* * *

Jackson Lanski woke in the decompression ward. Began to notice his surrounds and sighed. The mission was a success. The details faded as he lay there relaxing and decompressing. The Support staff attended him and closely monitored his progress.

Jackson walked out of his semi-private room and into the ward. He visited with the other patients of the ward.

He grabbed a handful of peppermint candy from the orderly station as he passed. He slipped peppermint candy to them as he continued on around the ward.

At last, he saw the one he was looking for. She sat in a wheelchair by the window. She stared out the window. Slowly, Jackson felt the panic rise. "No it can't be. This wasn't right."

He was back at The Institute. "NO! NO!" He moaned. She looked up at him and said, "Wakeup. Wakeup. It's all over. Wakeup."

Slowly Jackson's head cleared. Sylvie was holding his head in her lap. He was on the couch. His vision cleared. Wissle was on the floor of the cabin. He had a rough bandage on his shoulder. His hands and feet were tied with zip ties. He had a gag in his mouth.

"I could not listen to any more of his crap," said Lucy. She sat in a chair across from them. A bandage covered her forehead and right ear.

"What happened?" Jackson asked.

Sylvie answered. "The gas that put us out, stayed on this floor. It never made it up to the loft.

Lucy had only been conscious for a couple of minutes, when the guy came in the door, she yanked the trigger string to the shotgun. The buckshot hit him in the chest and head. He's still there by the open door."

Jackson checked the man by the door. His face was a mess. The gas mask had protected him from the gas, but not the shotgun blast. The BB's had broken the glass eye covers and driven the pieces into his eyes and on into his brain.

"We contacted your father, by Sat-phone. He's on his way in a helicopter with a cleanup crew."

Chapter 24: Back at Dad's

"Your daughters are safe Mr. Low."

"Thank you, Mr. Wang. I'm sorry about your nephew."

"Yes, it was an honorable death."

"He will be remembered." Mr. Low hung up the phone. He looked at his two daughters, Sylvie and Lucy in the frame side by side. "Someday I'll have to tell them."

* * *

It had been three months since the attack at the cabin. The Institute was shut down. Wissle was in jail. The doctor had disappeared, although, many thought him, dead.

"I don't know about you, but I'm sure glad to be back in your father's condo," Sylvie said.

She sat back in the over-stuffed chair with her legs crossed. Lucy sat in the other matching chair in the same position. Jackson lay sprawled on the couch. The TV was on. The late night talk show was on with the sound down low.

"What? Turn it up. Do you see that?" said Jackson. There, being interviewed by the host, was Boris, the Russian. "Turn it up. I want to hear this."

The Host smiled at Boris. "May I call you Boris?"

"Dah. Yes, my English is not good. Please excuse."

"Well it's fine. It's better than my Russian. So you have come to America and have asked for asylum. Is that correct?"

"Yes."

"And you already have a book in the works and a possible movie deal. Boy, that is the American dream."

"Yes, it is good to be in America."

" There you have it. The American Dream realized. We'll be back after this..."

"Well. Would you look at that? He will be alright," said Jackson.

"I'm glad I didn't kill him in the warehouse." Sylvie looked at Jackson askant, a coy glint in her eyes. "How about that shower, now? You ready?"

Jackson jumped up and headed for the bedroom. "You waiting on me?"

Chapter 25: Comeuppance

Doctor Einrich sat, tied to a chair with zip ties to wrists and ankles. In the dark, the sounds of dripping water and scurrying rats seemed amplified.

He could not see them, but he knew they were coming. The rats. A light came on. "Dr. Einrich, perhaps you should tell me what you think you are doing?"

Relieved, the doctor squinted into the glare. "Please, this is a bit clichéd. Really? The light. What do you want? Who are you?" He shook off the nightmare of the rats. "I have influence in high circles. You would do well to watch yourself."

"Yes, you did have. I'm afraid, they are the reason you are here. They have turned their backs on you." The doctor tried to see behind the light. "What do you mean? What do you want with me?"

The light went off. The sounds of dank damp and scurrying returned. "Wait. What have I done?" A low moan escaped, "Help." No response but the darkness.

Later, a voice in the dark spoke in a whisper. "Are you there? Can you hear me?"

Startled, the doctor cried out, "Who's there? What do you want?"

"Shh, they'll hear. Are you the doctor?"

"Yes, yes. Can you get me out of here?"

"Maybe. Can you help me? I have a slight identity issue. No one likes me. They're afraid of me."

"I have helped others with identity issues. I'm sure if you get me out of here, I can help you."

The doctor felt the speaker approach. He smelt his foul breath as he whispered, "I'll bite through the zip ties."

The light flashed on. There, way too close, was the image of a rat. Impossibly, a six feet tall, brown, shaggy and long naked tale, RAT! The light went out. The doctor screamed.

Later, the doctor regained consciousness. With the sounds of the dampness and scurrying away, as he became aware. In the dim light he could just see the windows across the room to his left. A lighter shade of gray squared in the wall.

In front of him was the light from last night. *Last night.* His eyes darted around the shadows of the room. No sign of anyone or thing.

"So, Doctor did you have a nice sleep?" The voice came from behind him.

"Wh... Who's there? What do you want with me?" he strained to see behind the chair.

"It's okay. You're safe. No one will hurt you." The giant rat jumped from behind the chair and put his face right in front of the doctor's. "Boo!" He sprayed a gas in the doctor's face.

* * *

"Is he ready?"

"Close, he might be ready for a trial run."

* * *

The doctor woke. He searched the white-walled room. He lay in a hospital bed. *The light was good*. He raised his arms. He brought his hands to his face. He needed a shave.

He got up off the bed and crept in to the bathroom.

He screamed, "No! No!" In the mirror where his face should be, was the face of a rat. He touched his face and the rat image followed suit, mimicked move for move. His hands were brown-skinned and looked like rat's paws with fur up his arms. He sank to the floor moaning, curled up in a fetal position.

* * *

"Using his own equipment to convince him he is a rat seems rather poetic."

"How long should we leave him like this?"

"Indefinitely. They'll let us know when to bring him out."

The second book in The Shadow Sweeper Series: *The Silver Shadow*, will be out soon. An excerpt from that book, follows.

Acknowledgments:

My wife, Audrey, for her patience, proofreading and support.

My son, J.T. for the cover design.

My grandchildren for being an inspiration to us all.

And the Good Lord for the ability and the time to write.

Thanks to the all readers who took a $0.99 chance on an unknown author.

About The Author.

Thomas Montgomery is a gentleman farmer, retired on a vast 1.63 acre ranch in east Texas. He lives there with his wife, Audrey, his dog, Bailey and his horse, Blaze and a bunch of guineas.

When he's not writing, he spends his time tinkering on old tractors and autos.

He hunts and fishes and all the other things a retired gentleman farmer would be expected to do.

Be among the first to know when I have a new book coming out. Email me at jacksonlanski@gmail.com and I will put you on my Newsletter list. No spam or busy emails will be forthcoming.

The Silver Shadow

Sylvie stood in front of the full length mirror. "This sucks. It makes me look like a hooker on Halloween. For God's sake. Who would want to wear this to their wedding?"

Lucy sat in a chair placed just for the purpose of an observer. "I wouldn't go that far. It does, however, seem a bit over the top. This is the... What, the tenth dress, you tried on and hated for different reasons. Really, some of them were very nice."

"Well, that one with the lacy bodice was kind of nice. I guess."

"I know. You'd get married in a running suit, if you had your way."

"Yeah, so? My mom has her heart set on making this a big deal." She started back into the changing room.

The crash of the large store front glass exploded in to the interior of the store. Intermingled in the glass and aluminum debris, a black SUV roared over and through displays of manikins in bridal gowns, white flowers and trellises.

The doors flew open. Four armed men in black, jumped out of the still moving vehicle. The rapid fire of automatic weapons raked the store.

In front of a viewing mirror, a young woman turned around. Shocked and indignant at the disturbance of her bridal gown selection day. It got worse.

She looked down at a blood red rose as it blossomed and grew in the center of the lacy bodice. She fell to the floor, posed poetically. The red stain spread onto the floor.

Store clerks and customers scattered and tried to hide. The chaos, a cacophony of killing spread through the store.

Future brides, no more. Only victims, now. Lost loved ones. Store clerks, also victims, now, lay like broken manikins.

The masked men marched through the store with military precision. They turned over the bodies that had tried to run away. They looked at each face. Then, on to the next sad obit. Business like and untouched by the slaughter.

Sylvie still in the hooker Halloween bridal gown, had grabbed Lucy and dropped behind the changing room wall. Lucy hand signaled that they go through the door into the storeroom. This was not their first firefight. Their training had kicked in when the first crash occurred. They were acting in concert.

Through the storeroom door, a man in black turned to face the sound of the door swinging in. Lucy came in hard and low. She hit him like a linebacker on a blitz. Except he never had the cup to protect his pride from Lucy's shoulder. His gun went off, into the air. The rifle fell to the floor. He lay groaning. Lucy picked up the rifle and shot him in the face.

His mission-buddy, alerted, came looking. He entered through the door. He called out in Mandarin,

"You good?"

Sylvie stood behind the door. Lucy turned from the man on the floor. He started to bring his rifle to bear on Lucy. Sylvie slammed the door into him. His shot was knocked askew. It hit Lucy in the side. Sylvie followed with a kick into his throat. He went down. She grabbed his rifle and ran to Lucy.

"Can you make it? We have to go."

Lucy got up from where the impact had dropped her. "I can make it," she groaned.

Sylvie helped her to the back door. The door alarm went off. They scrambled into the service corridor that ran behind the stores and out to a loading dock.

Sylvie slammed the door shut. She wedged the knife, she always carried, under the door. Lucy leaned against the wall. Her blood was starting to pool at her feet.

"We've got to stop this bleeding," said Sylvie, "Give me your knife." Sylvie took the knife and cut strips out of the five thousand dollar dress. "Let me see your wound."

Lucy lifted her blouse.

"It looks like it went straight through," said Sylvie as she packed in a folded strip and wrapped another strip around the waist to hold it tight.

The banging on the other side of the door signaled time to move. They were down to the first turn and almost around it, when shots rang-out. With a burst, they rounded the corner. Sylvie stopped. "Wait here." She stepped back, squatted low and looked back.

There were two men trotting toward the women. She sprayed some shots at them. More for effect than trying to hit them. Just to slow them down.

It worked. They hit the deck and got behind cover. They fired back, but Sylvie was gone. She had an arm around Lucy and was hurrying down the corridor.

At the end of the corridor, the big metal roll-up door was open and a truck was backed into the loading dock. They made it to the door as their pursuers came around the last turn.

Sylvie hit the button to lower the door. She fired back down at the men.

"What the hell?" said a man's voice behind her. She turned with her gun ready.

"Hold it. Hold it," he said with his hands up. "I don't want any part of this." He backed up. "I'll just be over here, out of the way."

Sylvie said, "You better be out of sight. The men chasing us will kill you, if they see you. Better run." The man took off, out past the truck and down the parking lot.

The plang, plang of the bullets pierced the door.

"Wait here," she said to Lucy. Sylvie hopped on to the forklift that had been used to unload the truck.

She looked at the controls. *Easy enough.* She started it up and swung it around and rammed into the overhanging door. The door was buckled. The forklift jammed into it, kept it from going up.

"Come on." She helped Lucy up. They hurried down the steps to the truck door.

Sylvie looked in and saw the keys in the ignition.

"Can you make it up and in?"

"I'll have to," she said and struggled up the truck step. Sylvie gave her an opportune shove that landed Lucy in the passenger seat, then ran around to the driver door, her ragged bloody wedding dress flapping behind.

She jumped in and studied the controls a moment. *Diesel with a Spicer 9 speed tranny.* She started the big rig.

"Come on. Come on," she said, as she waited for the air reserve to build and the emergency air brake to disengage and the tell-tale buzzer to stop.

The banging and rattling of the pursuers attempting to open the door, spurred her impatience. The banging stopped. *Uh oh, that's not good.* Sylvie saw a walk-through door a short way down the dock.

The buzzer stopped. She put the truck in low and with her foot on the brake pedal, pushed in the brake button. She let out the clutch and off the brake. The high torque of the diesel engine pulled the empty semi easily away from the dock. Sylvie shifted straight into third, then into fifth.

Continued soon in: *The Silver Shadow,* book two in *The Shadow Sweeper Series.*

If you would like to stay informed as to the progress of the series, go to my website at: www.sylvaniajackson.com.

On Amazon, a search under Thomas E Montgomery will connect you to the Author's page.

Updates and book releases will be posted at both sites.

Made in the USA
San Bernardino, CA
26 April 2014